Before I Knew You

ALSO BY CHARLENE CARR

A New Start Series
Skinny Me
Where There Is Life
By What We Love
Forever In My Heart
Whispers of Hope

Standalone

Beneath the Silence

Before I Knew You

CHARLENE CARR

Coastal
LINES

Library and Archives Canada Cataloging in Publication

Carr, Charlene
Before I Knew You / Charlene Carr

(Before I Knew You, Book)
ISBN: 978-1-988232-03-4

This novel is a work of fiction. Names, characters, places, and incidents either are the product of the author's imagination or are used fictitiously. Any resemblance to actual events, locales, organizations, or persons living or dead is entirely coincidental and beyond the intent of the author.

Typography by Charlene Carr

First Edition, July 2016

This work is also available in electronic format:
Before I Knew You
ISBN: 978-1-988232-04-1

For more information and a chance to join the author's Reader's Group visit:
www.charlenecarr.com

To the children long hoped for.

CHAPTER ONE

Joanna's heels clicked along the pristine tiles of her kitchen floor. Roast: fragrant and glistening. Another two hours would make it perfection. Potatoes: expertly seasoned in the slow cooker. A quick whipping and they'd be smooth and savoury. Vegetables: crisp green and wonderful. Her gaze scanned the room, searching for a stray crumb, a utensil out of place. She smiled. All was as it should be.

Her heels clicked into the front hall then grated to a halt. She leaned into the mirror, eyes wide, and pushed a stray hair back into place, smoothing it over and over until, finally, it gave in. She stepped back. Herself: flawless. On the surface, anyway. Her shoulders slumped slightly before she brought them upright again. Since the surface was all she could control, that's what she *would* control. She would bathe with the lavender oil Henry gave her for Christmas and delight in a manicure and pedicure. Then she'd really be perfect. Just as tonight would be. Just as the day they were commemorating was. Their wedding seemed like yesterday: June 20, 1974.

Thirteen years, and she could still smell the lilacs, could feel the sun's warmth on her face as she waited to walk through the garden and start her life with Henry. She'd been insistent on marrying the first day of summer. A day that held the promise of hope. Of sunshine, growth and love.

Thirteen years, and on the surface everything was perfect. Joanna's bottom lip quivered as she struggled to hold her smile. On the surface, everything seemed wonderful. Wonderful husband, wonderful house, wonderful life. Underneath, her life was a mess, an embarrassment. A failure.

She shook her head. But it didn't have to be, not forever. Tonight could be part of changing that. Tonight she'd smile and laugh and pretend they hadn't lost another child. Pretend everything was as it should be. And once they'd both sat in this fantasy long enough to believe it, to really believe they were happy and fulfilled, just as things were, she'd add to that joy by telling Henry she was ready to try again. This time it would work. It had to work. And less than a year from now they'd hold a child in their arms. Once again, it was time to hope.

In the bathroom Joanna tested the water with the back of her wrist, just as her nanny had always done. She stood back, enjoying the way the water cascaded down then burst into bubbles. Her head tilted. She turned off the water. Bang. Bang. Bang. The door. Who'd be knocking like that? A door to door salesman, probably. He'd leave if she waited long enough. But the banging continued. Joanna made her way to the front entry, looked through the glass, sighed, and pulled open the door. "Chrissy?"

"Oh, thank God you're home!" Chrissy thrust her squirming four-month-old, Tina, into Joanna's arms.

"Petey's got an earache. He's moaning and—"

"I can't watch her."

"If I take her to the clinic with Petey I'll have two sick kids on my hands." Chrissy's hair frizzed out on one side. Throw-up trailed down her shirt.

Tina gurgled in Joanna's arms. She let out a smiley burp. Joanna's chest constricted. "How long?"

"An hour. An hour and a half tops."

An hour and a half? Henry would be home and ready for dinner in two. "Not a minute longer."

"Thanks, doll!" Chrissy squeezed Joanna in a spastic hug. This wasn't the first time Chrissy had shown up frantic in the five years since she and her husband moved in next door, but still, her presumption was shocking. Joanna tried not to stiffen as Chrissy's arms wrapped around her.

"You can't be late. Henry and I have dinner plans."

"Dinner plans?" Chrissy laughed as she pulled back. "What's that again? Two adults, eating together, and no food gets on the floor?"

Joanna nodded, her lips tight.

"Don't worry. You'll get your dinner." Chrissy let a large bag plop to the floor. "She's fed. No worries there. Diapers and soothers and some of her favourite books and toys are in the bag." Chrissy pulled Joanna into another quick hug and turned away, her hand waving in a little 'too-da-loo' motion.

Joanna shut the door and gazed at the baby. That lavender scented bath was clearly not in Joanna's future. Perhaps a little spritz of lavender and Henry wouldn't notice the difference. But the manicure and pedicure? She held up her nails. They weren't horrible. Well shaped, though last week's polish had chipped in a spot or two—not that Henry cared about that kind of thing.

Joanna closed her eyes and held the baby close. She inhaled the scent—powder and lotion and something uniquely infant—a smell Joanna longed for. Better than lavender would ever be. Joanna could stand there all afternoon, lost in the scent of her. But the preparations had to continue. Joanna walked to the couch, grabbed several blankets, and laid them on the floor. The instant Tina was out of her arms the child whimpered. Joanna picked her up. Silence. She glanced at her nails again. Henry definitely wouldn't notice they were chipped. Even if he did, he wouldn't care. Joanna snuggled Tina against her chest. She kissed the girl's brow—soft and warm—then settled on the couch.

The dinner was prepped ... well, almost. Her clothes were laid out. Those were the things that really mattered. She pulled out her mental checklist, assessing the time each task would take and what she could let go of. Roast. Nothing to do there but baste it a time or two. Potatoes. They shouldn't take more than ten minutes to whip. Vegetables. Season and pop in the oven beside the roast ... she could probably do that with a baby in her arms or set the child down for a moment. Her outfit. Another ten maybe. And her hair? That would be tricky.

Tina stretched, her mouth opening to reveal a tender pink tongue. Joanna's shoulders relaxed. If this child was theirs, Joanna wouldn't worry about a perfect dinner or curling her hair. Maybe she would have taken Henry's suggestion to go easy on herself—let some chef cook their dinner. Probably she would have. But this wasn't their baby and Joanna had declined the offer of a dinner out. She wanted quiet. Calm.

Intimacy. The perfect environment to try again.

Joanna closed her eyes and sank deeper into the couch. Their baby, their most recent baby, would have been about two weeks old right now. Too young, certainly, for them to leave her. Joanna always believed she'd be the type of mother who handled it all—took care of her children and still had a hot meal waiting on the stove when her husband stepped through the door. She'd greet him—smiling, expectant—in a dress and heels, her hair perfectly coiffed. She knew it wasn't a life she had to lead—*The Feminine Mystique* had been out for over twenty years now—nor the life Henry expected, but it was the life Joanna wanted, the life she felt made for.

After about an hour on the couch Joanna snapped to attention. Dessert. She'd forgotten about dessert. She set Tina onto the blankets again. More whimpers. Joanna picked her up and Tina's whimpers turned into a wail. She sniffed the diaper then turned her head away.

Minutes later, in a new diaper and dressed again, Tina still wailed. Joanna's shoulders tensed. She jostled Tina in her arms and the cries rang louder. She stood and paced. Slowly, the crying eased, then ceased. Tina broke into a sleepy grin. Joanna couldn't help but laugh. She lowered Tina to the blankets once more, but before the girl even touched the ground, another wail. Joanna pulled her up.

One handed, she slid the vegetables into the oven, then walked some more. She looked to the clock. Time was running out. The potatoes lay un-mashed and still no Chrissy. The roast and vegetables finished, and still no Chrissy. Joanna wasn't dressed in the outfit she'd prepared, Henry's car pulled into the driveway, and still no Chrissy.

Joanna glanced out the window as Henry jogged up the

porch like a young man. She met him at the door. "What's this?" He grinned.

"Tina."

"Ah, Tina." Henry bent toward the little girl's face. She grabbed his finger and let out a squeal. He laughed, his salt and pepper hair shaking. "You didn't tell me we were having company for dinner." He kissed Joanna's temple.

"We're not." She explained the situation.

"You know as well as anyone you can't predict a wait at the doctor's office."

"I know, but—"

"It'll be fine." Henry reached for the girl. "How about you let me take her and you put the final touches on dinner."

The cries erupted the moment Tina transferred arms. Henry jostled and made faces, then passed Tina back to Joanna, a sheepish look on his face. "Okay. Maybe not."

"I wanted dinner to be perfect."

"Perfection doesn't exist."

How many times had Joanna heard that line? It may be true, but that didn't mean one shouldn't try.

Henry tilted his head, as if contemplating the situation. "I've got it. You hold the girl and I'll finish dinner."

Joanna rocked Tina. "You finish dinner?"

"If I can build a house I imagine I can finish a meal." He winked. "With direction, of course."

Joanna followed Henry into the kitchen and guided him. She strove to hold back a grimace as bits of mashed potatoes fell on the counter and kept her mouth shut as he sliced the roast against the grain. She almost stopped him when he put the vegetables on a plate instead of the serving platter she'd set aside. She bit her lip to keep quiet. Criticizing him would not be the way to start off their perfect evening, not that it could be perfect anymore. Bubbles of anger popped through her. This was just like Chrissy, like all of Joanna's friends really, to think nothing of asking Joanna to drop her plans in order to help them with theirs. Joanna who didn't have children, Joanna who didn't have a life. As if nothing she cared about could possibly matter compared to the concerns of being a mother.

Joanna's throat tightened ... but weren't they right? Guilt passed through her. Here she was putting a dinner over a sick child. She shook her head and pushed out a strong smile. "Should we start now? I'm sure I can manage with Tina on my arm."

Henry nodded as a knock sounded on the door. "Bet that's Chrissy now."

CHAPTER TWO

Joanna sat across the table from Henry. Just the two of them. Chrissy's husband had been at the door. Petey's ear infection sent Chrissy from the doctor's office to the hospital in Halifax. Another wave of guilt threatened to overtake Joanna, but she pushed it away. She had done the right thing. She'd watched Tina with a smile on her face … mostly. And Henry and her anniversary wasn't ruined. The food was a little cool, but edible.

Henry waved his fork after the first bite. "Now this would be the perfect reason to get one of those microwaves."

Joanna shook her head. "Food should be cooked in an oven."

He shrugged and spoke under his breath. "But it could be warmed in a microwave."

Joanna swallowed, self-consciousness spreading through her. She was still in her house pants and cardigan. "I planned to dress up."

Henry set down his fork. "You look great." He grimaced and ran a hand along his front. "And I didn't even change after work. Sorry, sweetie. I know you don't like me coming to dinner in my work clothes." He grinned. "Not too dust covered today though. I was mostly overseeing."

"It's fine." Joanna waved a hand.

"I can go change."

"The food will get even colder."

"Agreed." Henry picked up his fork. "You wanted to talk? That's why we stayed in?"

Joanna nodded. She looked to her plate. She'd wanted to enjoy the evening first. Enjoy the romance. But why put it off? She raised her gaze with a genuine smile. "I'm ready again."

Henry's fork paused mid-air. He set it down. "Joanna."

"It's been over six months now. The doctor advised we take that amount of time to think about this, decide whether we want to try again ... give my body a break in the meantime. I've had that break. I'm ready."

Henry stared at her. Joanna's smile faltered. She smoothed her shirt, though it didn't need smoothing. She let another smile blossom. "I thought maybe we could start tonight." Henry kept staring. "As good a time as any, don't you think? Our thirteenth anniversary and—"

"Yes. Thirteen years, Joanna. Thirteen years is enough."

"What do you—"

"I don't want to try anymore."

Joanna laughed—that tinkling one that came straight from her mother. "What are you talking about?"

"It's what you talked about. After the last time."

"After the—" Joanna remembered the words. Her words. She'd sat in the doctor's office, clinging to Henry. Sobbing. Five miscarriages. Five confirmed miscarriages. She suspected there'd been others. She never went to the doctor until she figured she was at least two months late. "I was upset."

"We both were."

"I didn't mean—"

"It sure seemed like you did."

Joanna sat straighter in her chair. "Well, I didn't. And I want to try again."

"No." He said the word with such strength. As if it was his decision and his only. Joanna glared at him. Her whole life people had decided for her, tried to tell her what she could and couldn't do. Other words came back to her. Words spoken in whispers in her hospital room after the first loss: *She's delicate. She's always been delicate.* And after the second: *Perhaps she has a poor constitution. She's tired so often, especially during her ... time.* Her mother's voice. *She's always been that way. Some women just don't handle being a woman as well as others.* And after the third: *Some women just aren't made to be mothers.*

They never said the words to her face, but said them in her hearing, as if she were deaf. They were the ones who were deaf—her family, the doctors—or who at least didn't know how to listen. Her whole life Joanna had tried to explain that something was wrong. She wasn't weak. She knew she wasn't weak. The crippling pain that visited month after month was intensely real. Not normal. The lethargy that accompanied that agony ... it didn't define her life, just parts of it, which meant, Joanna knew, it wasn't in her head like the doctors suggested. Tender. Delicate. She hated those words. Hated that people thought she should learn her limitations. And now, Henry, her one constant supporter, was saying the same thing.

His look of resolve softened to one of tenderness. "Not again, sweetheart."

Unlike her mother, her father, the doctors, Henry knew she wasn't weak, knew she wasn't prone to theatrics. All along he believed her when she said something was wrong. After the fourth loss, a loss that required surgery, the doctors told her what the problem was, a disease called endometriosis. A disease that explained all the 'crazy ladies' who insisted their 'women troubles' weren't normal. In a sense she'd felt vindicated, hearing that diagnosis. But she'd also felt victimized.

As if that diagnosis had sealed her fate, she didn't get pregnant again for seven years. Seven years of thinking she'd never have a child.

But then hope in the form of a new surgery that could help. She flew to the states for it. A slip of the scalpel and things had gone wrong. Death had loomed. But she'd recovered. Recovered, with no improvement. No change. Nothing for two years.

And then, like a miracle, nine years after her last miscarriage, it happened. She was pregnant. For three and a half glorious, hopeful months.

A half a month longer than she'd ever carried before. Which meant next time could be longer still. Next time it could work. Joanna leaned forward. "We can't give up."

"We have a good life, don't we?"

"Of course." Joanna took Henry's hand. "We have a wonderful life."

"Then be happy with that."

"I—"

"Jo."

She swallowed. "I can't—"

Henry pushed a hand through his hair. His voice sounded like gravel. "And I can't go through this again. Maybe you … but I can't." He paused. "You have to find a new dream."

Joanna squeezed his hand. "This is my dream. I was made to be a mother."

Henry looked to the ceiling. "You certainly had the touch with Tina today." He dropped his gaze to meet hers, the hint of a smile caressing his face. "You're good around children. You'd make an amazing teacher."

"Henry."

"Or maybe open a daycare."

"I have a job. I take care of you. This house. The business. The books."

"And you do it wonderfully."

Joanna released Henry's hand. "We've talked about this before. Being a teacher is a job. A great job. I know Carolyn," the words caught in her throat, "but I'm not Carolyn. It's not what—"

"It's not about Carolyn. And it's not about a job. It's about putting your mothering energy somewhere."

"Being a teacher is not being a mother."

"Of course not." Henry reached his hand toward hers. She pulled it away. "But maybe it's the next best thing."

"The doctor didn't say it's impossible."

"No." Henry pushed back from the table.

"It's cold. I know it's cold. I can put it in the oven." Joanna stood and grabbed the plates.

Henry grabbed her arm. "Maybe you can go through another loss like that, but I can't." He slackened his grip on her. Joanna kept her body turned from him. "You break more and more each time. It's like a part of you dies. Maybe you think you'll survive another," he dropped his hand, "but I can't survive watching it. I want you to be a mother. I want to be a father. I really do. But more than that I don't want to lose another wife. I can't."

Joanna turned back. "It won't kill me. I'm strong. I'm stronger than they say."

"It is killing you." He let the words hang in the air. "Maybe not physically, but sometimes I look at you and all I see is pain." He wrapped his hand around her waist. "Maybe if we let go, if we plan a different future, the woman I married, that happy woman, would come back."

"Henry." Joanna crouched beside him. "I'm happy. You make me happy. It's just—"

"Six babies, Jo. Six. I can't handle another."

Joanna let her head fall. Henry never spoke of his first wife. Never spoke of the child they'd lost. Since those first years of marriage, since Joanna's first miscarriage, if anyone brought up Carolyn's name, it was Joanna. Neither of them talked about the baby Carolyn had been carrying though. And so Joanna hardly thought of it. It was always five babies. Five losses. Joanna's losses.

But he'd had six. Seven, if you counted Carolyn. And how could he not count Carolyn?

Henry's voice—firm, quiet—broke the silence "It's too much."

Joanna nodded. She couldn't look at him but said the words he waited for. "Okay. Enough."

CHAPTER THREE

Joanna lay in bed long after Henry left the next morning. Even on her pain ridden days she got up, made Henry breakfast, packed his lunch, then started her day. Only when the pain was at its absolute worst, when any move shot stabs through her that felt like death, when she had to struggle to breathe, did she stay in bed. Today, though, the pain wasn't physical.

Henry had smiled when she said she'd sleep a little later and suggested he make a sandwich from the leftover roast for lunch. Rest up, he'd said, in that caring voice that cut to the core of her. He'd probably suspected her invisible disease was acting up. Poor, weak, fragile Joanna.

Joanna rolled over. That wasn't fair though, to think those were his thoughts. He'd never treated her like a burden. Never looked at her with that frustrating mix of sympathy and scepticism she saw in the faces of others. If they'd really known what she lived with, what she kept hidden, they'd be amazed. How many times had she made dinner, cleaned the house, entertained guests or gone to parties when any other person feeling what she felt would have stayed in bed? Countless.

Today though, she couldn't help it. At noon, with her head throbbing from lack of use and too many hours of closed eyes, Joanna emerged from her bedroom. The sun shone bright. The world outside her window looked radiant, inviting. It mocked.

Joanna only had one real dream growing up. One. It was a dream shared by almost every woman she knew. Though a few friends had aspirations that far surpassed motherhood or maybe didn't include it at all, motherhood was the standard, the ultimately attainable dream, so long as you found a man who was decent and kind. And Joanna found that man. Found him long before any of her friends. And yet the dream never came.

Now, with Henry's declaration, it was lost forever.

Once again, anger pulsed through Joanna. What did Henry expect her to do? Who did he expect her to be? She turned from the window. Who she had been, she supposed, for the past thirteen years. Or someone more. A teacher. A daycare worker. But she didn't want to care for other people's children. Teach other people's kids. On the side, for Henry, she was an accountant, bookkeeper, receptionist. Her real job though, what she considered her full-time job, was a homemaker. That's what she knew. That's what she wanted. Without a child though, without even the hope of one, there didn't seem to be much of a home to make.

Joanna scanned the house as she walked from room to

room. She'd done a thorough cleaning yesterday. The shelves and counters were dust free. The floor was vacuumed. After a quick swipe over the bathroom surfaces Henry had splashed as he shaved this morning, all glistened. She travelled to her desk and pulled open the binder in which she kept meticulous records of all of Henry's contracts. Everything was up to date. There was no one to call. Nothing to do.

If this bomb hadn't exploded in her life last night, how would she have filled today? She may have started a new Afghan, something soft and cozy. Perhaps gone to visit Chrissy or one of her other friends. The walking group was meeting today. There'd be a perfunctory question or two about Joanna's anniversary, and then talk of the children. Constant talk of the children. She couldn't bear it. Not today.

Joanna clutched her abdomen, almost wanting the pain—the cause of her barrenness. At least that would be a distraction. Henry was afraid another loss would kill her, but this death of hope ... with every other loss she'd still held hope. Now, hope dead, it felt as if every child she'd held within her, every dream she'd nurtured and believed in, was torn from her womb once more. The death of them all pierced her, over and over again.

Joanna turned back to the window and placed her hand against the glass. She'd have to clean the finger prints off later, but what did it matter? She had nothing better to do. The warmth of the sun flowed into her hand. Misery threatened. One dream. One. Who would she become without it?

She'd said it last night. She was *made* to be a mother, even if her body thought different. She knew it. Henry knew it. She'd felt it as she held Tina in her arms.

Tina. Tina, who meant more than a ruined dinner. Whose

soft skin and warmth pushed away the need for Joanna to fulfil her plans. Tina wasn't her child, and still it felt perfect. Still it felt right. Still it felt so good.

Joanna migrated to the couch and lowered herself. Maybe Henry had something with his idea of starting an at home daycare. Daily she could snuggle a baby in her arms, hear the pitter patter of feet running down her halls. Who would her clients be though? All the women Joanna associated with stayed home with their kids.

Even if she found children to look after, it would never work. Every day she'd risk feeling the loss she felt now. She'd grow to love the children and every night as evening came they'd leave, reminding Joanna that the joy they brought could never truly be hers.

Joanna stood. She pulled out the vacuum to clean a floor that didn't need it. The idea of a home daycare circulated through her mind. If only they could stay. If even one child could stay. A word she and Henry hadn't talked about since their first years of marriage floated before her. Adoption. She hadn't been open to it. How could she be open to it? She wanted her own child. She wanted a life growing inside her, a life she and Henry had produced through their love. She wanted those first flutters of movement, the first strong kick. In her five confirmed pregnancies she'd never gotten that far. Never once known for certain her child was active and moving around in there.

Joanna had brushed off adoption as a ridiculous notion. Nobody they knew adopted, unless it were a family member. She'd told Henry that the few times he'd brought it up in those first devastating years. Eventually, frustrated, determined her body *would* give her the child she longed for, she'd told him never to bring it up again.

But was it ridiculous? Surely babies were out there needing homes. Babies who wouldn't have to leave at the end of the day, who could be hers and Henry's only. Adoption.

Joanna switched off the vacuum. The part of her that had died last night was being reborn. Adoption! Through all their years of trying Henry had listened, had never brought up adoption again. Did he think of it though? Would he agree it was the way to make their dreams come true? Was it even possible?

Why wouldn't it be possible? Young women were getting pregnant all the time, weren't they? Women who wouldn't be ready to have a family. Her mother used to talk about it when Joanna was young: the scandals, the girls sent to boarding homes to have the child in privacy, the way they'd come back months later saying they'd visited a relative—though everyone knew the real story.

Of course, that was before the birth control pill had become legal, common. A number of Joanna's friends were on it, women who'd decided three or four children were enough. But could a young girl get it? A teenager?

Joanna thought back to her high school health class—In the late 60s and early 70s the overarching message was that nice girls would never have to worry about it. But plenty of nice girls got pregnant without meaning to.

Somewhere there must be a young woman who was waiting to give birth, looking for the perfect family to entrust her child to ... she and Henry could be that family.

Joanna wanted to shout her revelation, to call up her friends, to race to Henry. They could still have a baby. They could be parents. She dashed to his project files. He was at a site almost an hour away. By the time she'd travelled to tell him and come back home he'd be close to calling it a day anyway. But she wanted to do something. She had to do something. She could look in the phone book, find an adoption agency, get some information. She stopped. Would that be too much? Too forward a step to take without Henry's approval? The library. They would have resources. And there was nothing forward about merely researching. Joanna knew nothing about how these things were done, but she'd learn.

CHAPTER FOUR

Joanna was heading out the door when the phone rang. She returned to the kitchen, picked up the receiver, and twirled the cord around her finger. "Sampson residence. Joanna speaking."

"Joanna, precious. How are you today?"

"Mother, hello. I'm well. And you?"

"Just lovely." Her mother paused, a singular habit of hers, as if she were waiting an extra moment to ensure her listener was giving her complete attention. "I have a quick errand in your part of town. I'd like to stop by before for a cup of tea. Would arriving in thirty minutes be good?"

Joanna opened her mouth to protest—not that her mother's question was actually a question. She was coming. "That sounds wonderful. What has it been, a week?"

"At least. See you soon, darling."

Joanna hung up the receiver. The outfit she had on for the

library wouldn't do. After another quick look through all the main rooms—swiping a stray line of imaginary dust here, straightening a throw-pillow there, giving everything the keen eye of inspection she knew her mother would hold—she entered the bedroom and laid out a skirt, blouse, hose, and heels: an outfit her mother would approve of.

Ridiculous. To dress up for her mother! But better than suffering Marie's sly, disapproving glances, or worse, a seemingly caring comment. *Oh, are you having one of your difficult days, darling? You'll feel better if you spruce yourself up a bit. Or at least that's what I've always found.* If Joanna said she was feeling fine, Marie would let out a little huff. *Well,* some *women do dress more casually these days.* Joanna pulled up her hose and slipped into her heels. Certainly easier to change, even if it meant wearing shoes in the house— something she and Henry never did but that Joanna's mother thought was a sign of class.

After changing, Joanna touched up her makeup and waited for the doorbell. Marie's visits were sporadic and forceful. From time to time she simply came to 'catch-up'. To make herself feel like she was a good parent, Joanna guessed. But most of the time she had an agenda. Joanna hoped for a 'catch-up' day. Her mother was a good conversationalist. Delightful even. Joanna searched her memory, wondering if she'd given some perceived slight in the past few days, missed a family birthday or anniversary. Said something at their last gathering that her mother found offensive or low.

Marie had many good qualities. Joanna respected and emulated her mother's focus on order, cleanliness, always presenting oneself in the best light possible. In those ways, she strove to be like her. What she didn't respect was her mother's belief that her opinion should hold more weight than anyone else's—God and the Prime Minister included. If Joanna had offended her, after some pleasantries, Marie would deliver a slightly veiled lecture. Joanna's jaw clenched. She wasn't in the mood.

Several minutes later, Marie's gentle rapping sounded at the door. Joanna opened it to reveal her mother in a smart, perfectly fitted business suit. "Good afternoon, sweetheart."

Joanna leaned in for the light hug and air kiss beside her cheek. No use smudging lipstick, her mother used to laugh whenever Joanna tried to hug or kiss her as a child. Joanna air-kissed her mother back.

"How was your anniversary?"

"Very nice."

Marie pulled a card from her clutch. "From your father and me."

"Thank you." Joanna took the card.

"What did you do?"

"A quiet dinner at home."

"Oh?" Marie's brows raised. "Is Henry having trouble?"

"Not at all."

"Because if he is, your father could help, get him some larger contracts or—"

"He's fine." Joanna gulped at her mother's sharp look. Marie hated being interrupted. "I thought an intimate setting at home would be nice. I set candles." She hadn't, but she'd planned to—that was close enough to the truth as need be.

"Well," Marie passed through the entry and into the living room, "*Mario's* has candles too."

"I know. I just ..." Joanna sat on the couch across from her mother. The tea lay waiting, but Joanna didn't pour it. "I thought it'd be nice, more intimate to have a quiet dinner at home." Joanna hesitated. Should she tell her mother? She wanted to tell someone, though she could guess what Marie would have to say ... Anything that wasn't traditional was automatically taboo. "I was hoping to convince Henry it was time for us to try again."

"Oh, Joanna." Her mother laid her perfectly manicured hands across her lap. Joanna folded her own so Marie's eyes wouldn't search out the slight chips in her polish. "Don't you think enough is enough? Every time you try it's so stressful."

"I know but—"

"You're my only girl and watching you so hopeful, and then the way you sink into such misery after."

"I don't—"

"It's very unpleasant to witness."

Joanna sucked in a cool stream of air. Of course that's what her mother would focus on, how unpleasant it was for *her*. Marie nodded to the tea. Joanna poured a cup for her mother, adding one teaspoon of sugar and a splash of cream, just as Marie required it.

Marie took a sip. "I know being a mother is important to you, but sometimes in life we have to accept our fate. I was hoping for two boys and two girls but I got your three brothers before you came along. You don't see me complaining."

"Yes, but—"

"And all of this is distasteful to even talk about. You've done very nicely for yourself." Marie cast her gaze around the room. "You know your father and I had our reservations when you decided to marry a carpenter. That was not in our plans either. But you have a nice home, a respectable home, and though a little uncouth at times, Henry is a delightful man."

Joanna pressed her lips together. Henry was a contractor. He did carpentry. But he was also a contractor, owner of an established business. Not that there was any point in stressing that fact. The distinction made no difference to Marie. At least she'd called him delightful.

"He's stood by you, and that's more than many men might do when faced with your," Marie smoothed her skirt, "problems." She cleared her throat. "You should be thankful for that. Pursue other interests if that may help. Some advisory boards, perhaps. I know the hospital was looking."

"I don't want to join an advisory board."

"Then join something else." Marie waved a hand. "I keep my days busy. Of course I have your father's social calendar to manage, but ... oh," Marie's smile brightened, "the Salvation Army is looking for a new events planner for the local branch. I bet you'd be perfect at that."

"Mother."

"Yes."

Joanna bit her lip. She'd gone this far ... time to hope for the best. "I'm thinking of adoption. I haven't talked to Henry yet but—"

"What?"

"He can't handle another miscarriage. He doesn't think I could handle it, along with the stress of trying to get pregnant ... but with adoption we wouldn't have to worry about that."

Marie took another sip of tea. "I hope you're joking."

"It would mean we could have a child, our own child—"

Marie sighed, her expression the one she reserved for people who just didn't understand. "It wouldn't be your child. It would be someone else's."

"I know, but—"

"Do you even know anything about this? Babies don't just grow on trees."

"Of course not."

Another sip. "You need to accept your fate, darling. Truly. I speak this with all love."

Joanna sat, staring. This was ridiculous, the way her mother, with a single word, a single glance, could make her feel like a child again. She wasn't a child. She was a thirty-three year old woman. A woman who could make her own decisions, who didn't need her mother's approval. She straightened her spine. "I'm not asking for your blessing or even your opinion."

Marie set her tea down. "Then why did you bring it up?"

Why did she? Even growing up she never talked to her mother about personal things. The nanny received all of Joanna's secrets. But the nanny was long gone. "You're my mother."

"Which is why you should trust me. This is not the answer."

"But it could be. Don't you think it could be?"

"Where would this child come from, Joanna? What decent person gives up their baby?"

"Girls get in trouble."

"Not the decent ones."

"Mother, you're so—"

"What? What am I?"

Joanna wavered. Snobby. Old fashioned. Close minded. She leaned forward. "It wouldn't be the child's fault. And if we raised it from a baby ..."

Marie reached for her tea. Her pinky raised slightly, as did her left eyebrow. She looked at Joanna, unshakable as a mountain, and said nothing.

"Maybe father would know people. Or could help. Has he ever worked a case where—"

"Your father is in Acquisitions."

"His friends may have though? I'm guessing lawyers would have to be involved. And—"

Marie gave another sigh—the one she reserved for indulging someone she felt was acting like a delusional child. Joanna had received it countless times in her youth. "If you insist, I will ask him. He will say no, he can't help, I'm sure of it. But I will ask."

"Thank you."

Marie offered the slightest of smiles. "This is a bad idea. And it won't be easy."

"It can't be harder than what we've been through."

Another sigh. "If it's very important to you," Marie stressed the word very, "and if you insist, we'll see what we can do to help. Perhaps a baby from a good family whose parents have died."

Joanna bit her lip to keep from reacting. "Thank you, Mother."

Marie looked away. She placed a finger on the centre of her lips. "Car accidents do happen." She set her cup down and brought her gaze to Joanna. "That wouldn't be so terrible. It'd even be ... noble." Her smile grew and her chest rose. "Admirable. Rescuing a child like that." Her smile faded. "Though, most likely there would be some family wanting to take the child in that circumstance." Marie shook her head. "Whether you want my opinion or not, here it is. This is risky business, Joanna. You have no idea what you could be getting yourself into."

"I'd be getting into another chance to be a mother." Joanna paused and leaned forward. "Just imagine. Imagine how you would have felt if you never got to be a mother."

Marie wore a new smile now, the one most typically seen at social events. Of all her smiles, this was the most stunning. "Of course, my dear. You and your brothers are my pride and joy." The smile transitioned slightly, the corners of her lips sinking a fraction. "Just be cautious. Hopeful, but cautious."

CHAPTER FIVE

Hopeful but cautious. Those words pretty much defined Joanna's whole life. After watching Marie's car reverse and peel out of the driveway, Joanna checked the clock. There wasn't nearly enough time to get to the library and back home again before Henry arrived. But she needed some distraction to put her mother's words out of her mind. This was an exciting prospect. She wanted to be excited! Surely, to Henry, this would be the answer they'd both been waiting for. He wouldn't mind if she took the first steps. Joanna picked up the phone book and rifled through the numbers. She tried three, though none of the names sounded quite like what she was looking for. On the fourth call, a woman picked up.

"Family Foundations, how may I help?"

"Hello." Joanna put on her most professional voice. "This is Joanna, Joanna Sampson. I'd like to speak with someone about adopting a baby."

Joanna waited as she was transferred to another line. A woman named Meverly introduced herself then asked Joanna several perfunctory questions: Were she and her husband legally married? Did her husband work? Did she? Did they have any children? Had they tried to have children? "These things are better discussed in person," Meverly finally said, as if apologizing.

"I could come in any time."

"We'll have to set up a home visit. We don't just give children away to anyone."

"No, of course not." Joanna laughed. "That would be ridiculous. You're welcome to come just about any time."

"I don't like going out of my way for no reason. Are you serious about adoption or is this just an option you're exploring?"

Joanna hadn't even talked to Henry yet, but he'd be on board. All those years ago it'd been him to bring up adoption. She had brushed the idea away. "We're serious. We've decided."

"You've decided based on what you know." The woman sounded tired. Overworked. "If you're really serious though, rather than you coming here and then me going there, it will save time for me to come to you. Coming to the office would be a waste of time if the home visit doesn't go well."

"I don't see any reason why it—"

"If you'd been doing my job as long as I have, you'd see reason."

"I see." Joanna straightened her skirt. If this woman cut her off one more time ... well, Joanna would do nothing. She needed this woman. "Come any time. Just let me know. I'm at home so—"

"Your husband needs to be there too. We meet both prospective parents."

Joanna pressed her lips together. "No problem. Any evening but Thursday would be—"

"I only do home visits in the morning."

"Well, then." Joanna rushed to Henry's day planner. He was busy every day for the next two weeks at least. "I'll have to check but I'm sure we can work it out."

"Call me when you do."

Joanna could tell by the woman's voice she was about to end the call. "Wait. What should I do in the meantime? Is there anything to prepare?"

"To prepare?" The woman paused. "You want a baby, correct? A newborn?"

"Most definitely."

"You realize it's you as an adoptive parent who'll be on a waiting list, not the newborn."

"I imagined that."

"That's all you do. Wait. Call me when you're ready to set up a visit and we'll talk more."

"Well, all right then."

"Have a good day."

The woman hung up the phone before Joanna could even thank her and say goodbye. She stared at the receiver. No matter. The woman may be gruff, but she was also Joanna's avenue to finally becoming a mother.

When Henry walked in the door, Joanna was waiting for him. "Good day?" She took off his coat and went up on tip toes for a kiss. With almost a foot between their heights, Joanna loved how dainty she felt in his arms.

"Pretty good." He sighed and rubbed a hand along her shoulder. "I was worried though. How are you feeling?"

"I'm great. Fabulous."

"Fabulous?" Henry tilted his head. "The pain's eased up?"

Rather than explain, Joanna nodded.

"And ... well," he let out a little sigh, "I know last night's decision was hard for you, but once we both accept it we'll be a lot happier. Maybe we can take a trip. Back to Europe. Or even Asia." He squeezed her shoulder again.

"I made a new decision today." Joanna grinned. "A decision that makes last night's decision a little less awful. A way we can still be parents."

Henry walked through the hall and into the living room. He sat on the couch and looked up at her. "I was serious about what I said."

"I know." Joanna sat across from him. "I want to adopt."

"Adopt?" Henry leaned forward, his long legs spread. "We haven't talked about that in years."

"I know."

"And we decided—you decided it's not what you wanted, that you wanted your own baby."

Joanna sat straighter. "And you decided that won't happen. So this can. This will."

"Do you know anything about adoption?"

"I called an agency. As soon as you can find a morning to take off we'll book an appointment."

"We'll book—" Henry stood. "You called? Don't you think this is something we should talk about first?"

"We are. Right now." Joanna stood too, she gripped his hands. "This way we get what we want and avoid what we don't. A healthy baby. A child to call our own. No months of fruitless trying. No miscarriages."

Henry paused. He looked away then turned back, grinning. "I'd put the idea aside. Completely. I stopped thinking about it."

"Me too."

"An appointment, huh? To get more answers, learn what this is all about?"

"Exactly. To start the process."

"It could be complicated. It could not even be possible."

"Of course it's possible." Joanna tutted. "People have unplanned babies, and those unplanned babies need homes." She passed Henry the day planner. "Find a morning."

Henry replied without looking at the pages. "This contract's tight. It'll be at least two weeks."

"Two weeks." Joanna pushed out a smile. "What's two weeks after thirteen years? Pick a date and I'll set up an appointment."

Henry laughed. "You're really gung-ho on this. Aren't you?"

"Why shouldn't I be?" Joanna stepped back. "We're letting go of something big. The dream of our own baby— direct from me and you. But holding Tina yesterday ... once a child was in our home, once we knew he or she was here to stay. That child would be ours, don't you think?"

Henry crossed the distance between them, scooped her up and spun her. His laugh sent darts of warmth from her fingers to her toes. "I think this is the best news I've heard in years."

CHAPTER SIX

On the morning of the home visit Joanna woke up early. In the two and a half weeks since her initial call to the agency, she'd borrowed and read every book the library had on adoption, which, to her dismay, wasn't many. But she'd learned a few things. Already, she'd designated a room for their future child. They'd been eager the first time Joanna was pregnant, excited, and had gone out and purchased a crib, rocking chair, change table, an assortment of neutral coloured baby clothes and stuffed animals. It'd been foolish really. She'd been barely three months along when she miscarried ... but back then losing a baby wasn't a possibility she'd even considered. Neither had Henry, at least not in that way.

In the years in between the items stayed carefully packed in their back shed, draped over by layers of painter's tarp. Out of sight, but never out of mind. When Joanna retrieved them she held each item before designating its new spot. She could remember purchasing every one, remember the excitement, the joy. Should she have named each lost child? She hadn't, though sometimes wished she had.

She brought in all the small items on her own, slowly, trying to transfer the hope she'd held for each one into a new kind of hope. Hope for the new child she'd welcome into her life.

She needed Henry's help to bring in the furniture. He didn't like the idea. What if something went wrong? he asked, what if it didn't work? Joanna had paused, smiled. What if it helped things go right? For them to show they were ready, invested, could only bode well for their home visit, or so the books she'd read said.

The books had also talked about potential issues— behavioural, attachment disorders, etc. But most of that seemed more likely with older children, children who remembered their parents, who realized they'd been abandoned or torn away from the mother and father they'd loved ... Joanna's dream was of the next best thing to delivering her own child—receiving one hours after the baby had taken its first breath. So long as the mother was healthy, Joanna couldn't imagine any other problems arising. Of course, one day they'd have to tell the child where he or she really came from, but the books suggested to frame the situation around love—love of the biological parent in knowing she couldn't provide the best life for the child, and love from her and Henry, for choosing this baby to become a part of their family. The child could still rebel, but it'd be less likely.

After checking the prospective baby's room to ensure everything looked inviting, Joanna scanned the rooms she'd cleaned the day before. She'd already prepared chocolate chip cookie dough and popped the spooned out batter into the oven so the scent would give a sense of home. This hadn't been in an adoption book, but she'd read it in a house and home magazine as a trick to make prospective buyers feel more comfortable and welcomed. It should work for today too. Anything to make it clear this was a home a child would thrive in. After getting herself ready, Joanna fussed with Henry's tie.

"Do you really think I need this?" He pulled at the fabric. "Isn't it a visit to see what our home environment is like? I never wear ties at home." He tugged again. "I never wear ties at work."

"You wear them during business meetings." Joanna adjusted Henry's collar.

"Yeah, once or twice a year."

"We want to appear respectable."

"We are respectable." Henry tugged again. "Isn't it more important to appear genuine?"

Joanna brushed a piece of fluff off of Henry's jacket. He looked good in a suit. Dapper. She didn't begrudge how rarely he wore them though. She'd married a contractor, not a lawyer. "Just for today. We'll be making our first impression. Let's have it be a good one."

Henry nodded. He bent and kissed her forehead. "As soon as this woman leaves, it's coming off." He sniffed the air. "Cookies? For breakfast?"

Joanna laughed. "The smell of cookies—to add to that wonderful impression we'll be making."

At quarter to ten Joanna did one last walk through the house. She paid careful attention to the rooms they rarely used ... one of them may be full soon. At ten fifteen Joanna and Henry sat in the living room, waiting.

"The woman said she'd be here at ten?"

"At ten, yes." Joanna tapped her foot. "She may have gotten lost or held up. Anything could have happened."

"That's true." Henry shifted. He looked at his watch.

Joanna uncrossed then recrossed her legs. Henry had to be at the work site by twelve. It was almost an hour away. If he looked rushed, Meverly may interpret it as seeming un-invested.

"Well, she's not making the best impression." Henry stood. "I might as well go over the plans for today. The owner decided he wants a reading room, so we'll have to resize the bathroom and hall closet."

Joanna stayed seated. She reached for her knitting. A tiny blanket with soft wool in a pale green. For the first time in a long time she worked the needles with the expectation that this item would be staying right here, instead of gifted to someone else with exciting news.

At ten twenty-four a knock sounded. Joanna sprang from her seat. She rushed to the entry then stood waiting as Henry strode toward her. She opened the door. The woman who stood on the porch was in her mid-fifties. Short, shorter than Joanna even, stout, with graying hair pulled back in a tight bun. Glasses rested on top of her head. She wore a three-quarter length dress suit, which made Joanna pleased with her similarly styled outfit.

"You must be Meverly." Joanna beamed. "Come in, come in."

"I apologize for being late."

"Oh, that's all right." Joanna retreated further inside to

give Meverly space to enter. "We're just so glad you're here. I'm Joanna, and this is my husband, Henry."

Henry reached out his hand. "It's nice to meet you, Meverly. I have to be off around eleven. So any questions you need to ask of me should maybe come first."

Meverly nodded as she entered. "That should be fine." She stepped further in. "This is a lovely home you have."

"Henry built it."

"With the help of my crew."

"Don't be modest." Joanna laughed and gestured to Henry. "He designed it and built it. He owns a construction company." She turned back to Meverly. Would you like a tour before or after we sit down for a chat?"

Meverly pulled out a clipboard and slid her glasses onto her face. "We'll start the chat on the tour."

Joanna led Meverly down the hall and toward the bedrooms. Henry trailed behind. "In addition to the master, we have three extra rooms." She stepped into the first. "Obviously we don't need this much space. We were hoping for a large family. This I use as a knitting room, but that's entirely unnecessary."

"You had trouble conceiving?"

Was the woman not listening when Joanna told her this on the phone? But of course she probably talked to so many women. "Trouble conceiving, and when we did conceive, trouble carrying the babies to term."

"That's often the case." Meverly nodded. "I'm sorry for your loss."

"Thank you." Joanna squeezed Henry's hand as he rested it on her shoulder. "Now this room," she said as they walked into the next, "had been laying empty for quite a while, but as you can see we've already prepped it for a child, in case an opportunity arose quickly."

"That's not likely." The woman looked to her clipboard again.

"But it's always good to be prepared."

"True." Meverly opened her mouth to speak then closed it. Joanna stared, waiting.

"And to hope." Joanna said when Meverly kept quiet. "Henry and I know all about hoping."

"How long did you say you'd been trying?"

"Thirteen years."

"Thirteen?" The woman scratched something on her paper again. "And this is the first time you've considered adoption?"

"The first time we seriously considered." Joanna glanced to Henry then back to the woman.

"Like Joanna said, we were hopeful. But the losses, the repeated losses, we decided we needed to stop trying for our own baby."

"And then I thought opening our home to a child in need would be the next best thing."

"And you want a newborn?"

"We do."

After pointing out the other two rooms, the Master, bath, backyard, and kitchen, Joanna motioned for Meverly to sit in the living room. Joanna and Henry sat on the love seat, hands clasped. Joanna's pulse quickened—the look on the woman's face ... not good.

Meverly looked to her notes once more. "Joanna, you are how old?"

"Thirty-three."

"And Henry?"

"Almost forty-seven."

"That's a big difference."

Joanna leaned forward. "Is that a problem?"

"Not necessarily. Not in itself. Oddities often make prospective mothers a little weary. They tend to favour younger parents. Henry's age may increase your wait."

"That doesn't seem fair." Joanna squeezed Henry's hand tighter. "He's a healthy man. Vigorous. And forty-seven is still young."

"Yes, but you seem to think this is a quick process. It can be, but it can also take several years. Four. Five. Maybe longer. Often longer."

Joanna clenched Henry's hand tighter. "I wasn't aware."

"That's if you want a newborn. Everyone wants a newborn."

"So it's just a matter of waiting in line?"

"To a degree." Meverly gave a little sigh. "It's a complicated process. Birth parents, usually just the birth mother to be honest, can jump the queue, in a sense. But we encourage them towards those who've been waiting longest. If you'd put your name on the list years ago, when you realized there was a problem ..."

"Well, we didn't." Henry wrapped an arm around Joanna's shoulder. "So no point worrying about that now."

Joanna looked between Henry and Meverly. "It doesn't make sense that age would—"

"It's more than that. The mothers will have a right to know a bit of your background, how long you've been trying, etc." Meverly closed her lips and inhaled. She looked like a schoolmarm. "It may not bode well that you've just applied for adoption. It could indicate a resistance to the idea. No one wants to believe their child will go to a family who views them as second choice, the next best thing."

"But—"

"I'm not saying that's how they'll view you." There the woman went, cutting Joanna off again. "I'm just saying it's possible. I want to prepare you for the ways in which things could go wrong."

Henry pulled his arm away from Joanna and leaned forward. "What other ways could things go wrong?"

"Sometimes mothers change their minds months, weeks, days before the birth."

"But wouldn't there be some agreements in place or—"

"It's not like the past, when babies were smuggled away. These girls have rights. They have all the rights in these situations. It is their child."

"I suppose ..." Joanna looked to Henry. "I suppose that makes sense."

"Sometimes they request to hold the baby for a few minutes after the birth, and in those minutes they realize they can't let the child go after all." Meverly removed her glasses and set the clipboard on the chair beside her. "At that point you could be ready. You could be in another room eager to meet your child only to learn he or she won't be your child after all. Many find it devastating. Most. You've already been through a lot of loss. This could be more loss—again and again."

"Does it happen often," Henry's knee bounced, "mothers changing their minds?"

"Often enough. Legislation allows a contemplation period. Mother's have up to twenty-one days after they've given up custody to change their mind. You could take the baby home, start to love it, and then have to say goodbye."

"That's—" Joanna swallowed. "I had no idea."

"It's a scary period. It doesn't happen often, mother's changing their minds after the child has gone home with the adoptive parents, and it would need to be determined by a judge that the mother was in a healthy state of mind and able to provide for the child, but it does happen." Meverly folded her hands, her lips pressed together, schoolmarm-like once more. "It's more than that. Costs are associated with this process. Lawyer's fees, assessment fees. If the mother changed her mind any costs you'd incurred up until that point would also be lost. This isn't a quick and simple solution to having a family. Not at all."

"It sounds like you're trying to deter us." Henry's voice was hoarse. "Don't you want people to adopt?"

"When it comes to couples open to newborns ... to children up to two years old actually, we have more than enough couples ready and eager. I need to make sure they're ready and eager even after knowing all the risks and potential heartache."

"Up to two years—"

"If you're willing to go that old it would increase your chances somewhat. You have a lovely home here. Your husband owns his own business?"

Henry nodded.

"And you are a homemaker, Joanna?"

"Yes."

"All that is in your favour."

Henry rubbed a hand along his jaw. "And why two years old? Why does that age make a difference?"

"Children under two are less likely to fully comprehend the situation they're in—being separated from their parents, going to a new home. They understand a change of course, there can be a lot of stress involved in that, but they can't express that stress in a cognitive way. Also, they're likely to forget their old families eventually, form more solid attachments to their adoptive families."

"That makes sense, I suppose." Joanna looked to Henry, she rubbed her hand along her forearm. "Doesn't it?"

"It does."

"Would you be open to expanding the age to two years old?"

"I don't know." Joanna looked to Henry again.

"We'd have to discuss it."

"Of course." Meverly slid her glasses on and picked up her clipboard. "I recognize you have to leave soon, Mr. Sampson. If you decide to go forward with this you'll both need to undergo psychological assessment to determine you're in a healthy state of mind, suitable to adopting a child. You'll also need to have police and medical record checks done. Take a few days to think, to talk, and if you decide to, call me back to book your appointments."

"A psychological assessment?" Joanna hesitated. "So we could be deemed unsuitable?"

"It's possible." Meverly offered a smile, her first real one since she'd stepped in the door. "From what I've observed of you so far, I don't imagine there'll be a problem. That step in the process is certainly the least to be concerned about."

"And it could be years?" Henry rubbed a hand down his pant leg. "But less if we were willing to take an older child?"

"It could be less. There are no guarantees."

CHAPTER SEVEN

Henry closed the door behind Meverly. "No guarantees." He turned to Joanna. "That's exactly what we were trying to avoid." He pushed a hand through his hair. "This could be everything we've lived through for a decade, all over again."

Joanna bit her lip. "Not exactly. It wouldn't hold the physical stress, the trying to plan, the fear of miscarriage, the," she hesitated, "it wouldn't be the same. Not really."

"No." Henry stepped away from the door. "Not exactly. But similar. It sounds like ..." He offered a gentle smile. "It sounds like this is something we may want to think deeply about before pursuing."

"But what other choice would we have? It's this or nothing."

"Not nothing." Henry reached for her hand. "We wouldn't have nothing."

"But no children. Ever."

"Let's take some time to think." Henry looked to the clock. "I need to get going, but lets both of us just take some time to think."

Joanna went to their home office when Henry left. She had work. As Henry's current job was nearing completion, another one would start soon. She had contracts to look over, numbers to crunch. She sat at the desk and flipped through the pages. What first? Meverly's warnings filtered through her mind, pushing out all thoughts of contracts.

Could she handle it? To believe they were days away from having their baby, minutes even, and have all those hopes torn away? Or, even worse, to take a baby home, to hold a precious new life in her arms, and then to have to say goodbye? Terrifying. Even if it never happened, just the fear that it could ... Not easy. Not for her and not for Henry.

Even with all the loss Joanna had gone through, Henry had experienced more. She didn't like to think about his first wife, but not thinking about her didn't erase her existence. She'd been beautiful. Vivacious. The type of woman to make people stop and stare. Joanna still remembered the first time she'd seen Carolyn. A music teacher at the high school, Carolyn had walked into Joanna's classroom with a large smile on her face. Joanna, in her final year, had been captivated. The way Carolyn spoke, the way she moved. She was everything Joanna wanted to be and wasn't. Joanna was reserved, shy, insecure. Not the type of woman a man would notice. When Carolyn walked into a room, heads turned.

That's the biggest reason Joanna didn't like to think about Carolyn. She couldn't compare. Joanna knew Henry loved her—never doubted it for a minute. But she couldn't see how Henry had gone from loving someone as dynamic and outgoing as Carolyn to loving someone as reserved as her.

Of course, Carolyn's adventurous spirit had killed her, her and the baby she carried. Maybe that's why Henry had chosen Joanna. She was safe. With her there wouldn't be that kind of heartache ... or so he had thought.

Because of Joanna and her damaged body, Henry had endured heartache after heartache through the years.

Adoption was a way to stop that. Adoption could give him, them, a family. He'd made his stance clear about trying to get pregnant again, so it was adoption or nothing, and Joanna couldn't accept nothing, not without trying every avenue.

In need of a distraction, Joanna spent the majority of the afternoon working on the business. It should have only taken a couple of hours. But the tasks weren't distracting enough. Meverly's words bombarded her thoughts, causing her to double and triple check numbers and lines of texts.

By the end of it, Joanna had made a decision. When Henry arrived home, she would assure him adoption was worth the risk, that it was a risk less intense than the ones they'd been taking for years. That they had to believe.

"Have you thought about this morning?" Joanna asked after serving their plates that night.

Henry laughed. "Almost exclusively."

"Really?" Joanna sat across from him. "Me too. And?"

"And everything seems stacked against us. It was naive, obviously, but when you presented this idea I thought it would be a sure thing. I thought this route could make us parents. I didn't think there'd be such uncertainty. Such risk."

"Me neither."

"And there's a lot of risk."

"I still want to try."

Henry rubbed his chin. "I figured you would. But we'd just be going down the same path we've been on before."

"The baby wouldn't be dead. If we thought we were getting a child and then lost that hope, at least we'd know the child would still live."

Henry twisted his glass back and forth on the table. "That's true."

"There'd be no physical trials for me. No close calls."

"It's the emotional trials too though. I hate seeing you so sad."

Joanna sat straighter. "Life can be sad. But we're strong. After every loss we still got out of bed. We still made it through the day. We still had each other."

"You're strong." Henry sighed. "I don't know how much more strength I have."

"Enough." Joanna smiled. "I'm sure of it. You have enough. We both do."

"And if it doesn't happen? If we go years and years and—"

"Then it's no different than the situation we'd be in otherwise." Joanna reached her hand across the table. "We can live our lives. We can be happy with each other."

"I don't want this to become an obsession, to always be waiting by the phone. To have a constant hope."

Joanna looked to the table. Could she do that for him? Not be obsessed? Probably not. But she could hide it. Maybe, after time, she could relax. "We could take the first steps, get things in place, and then view it as a possibility." Joanna took a breath. "Not something we base our lives around but something we're open to."

Henry's head fell. He rubbed his hands through his hair.

His chocolate brown eyes looked so vulnerable. "Do you think we can do that? Honestly?"

Joanna stared at him, her heart thumped against her chest. "We can try. Maybe trying will be enough."

"You remember when we were happy?" Henry leaned his elbow on the table and his head in his hand. "When just the two of us seemed like enough?"

"We always wanted children."

"But when we thought we'd have them, it was different."

Joanna pushed back from the table. She stood. "Can we start the process? Set up the assessments? Be open?"

Henry's nod was slow. Uncertain. "If that's what you want." His brows pulled inward. "But this terrifies me."

Joanna stared at Henry. The best man she knew. Full of love. He deserved to be a father. Needed to be, whether he realized it or not. And if his hopes were raised and dashed all over again because Joanna had to keep trying, could she forgive herself?

She walked around to Henry, then laid a hand on his shoulder. "It scares me too. But just think, a baby. If the bad stuff doesn't happen, and we have no reason to think it will, we could finally have our baby."

CHAPTER EIGHT

The next day Joanna called Meverly to let her know they wanted to set up the assessment with the psychologist. Tomorrow she would go to the police station and contact their doctor for the medical records. The soonest psychologist's appointment was almost three weeks away.

"That's fine." Joanna smiled into the phone. "No problem at all." Over the next week Joanna did her best to go about life as normal. She kept up the house. She kept up with Henry's books. She visited her friends and family. Her mother knew their plans, but beyond that she didn't see a reason for anyone else to. Henry and she didn't talk about the adoption—all the challenges and possibilities it could bring— beyond Joanna telling him the appointment date. That was the unspoken deal. Go about life as if this may never happen; remain open to the idea that it could. It was all working out. It *would* all work out.

After the first few days, however, Henry seemed agitated. "How's the new job going?" Joanna asked as they sat in the living room after dinner one night.

"Good." Henry focused on the wood carving he held in his hand.

"It's a complicated design, right? The house?" Joanna picked up her knitting.

"Mmhmm." Henry's head stayed down.

Joanna watched the wood shavings fall to the floor around Henry's feet. She hated the mess but loved the intricate creations. "Good crew?"

"Fairly good." The corner of Henry's lips twitched in an almost smile. "One young fella could probably do to be put in his place. Thinks he's a rock star."

"Will it be a problem?"

Henry chuckled but kept his gaze on the piece of wood. "Wouldn't be surprised if one of the older fellas takes care of his big head sometime soon."

Joanna nodded. Despite this chuckle, something was off. Henry had hardly looked at her all night. Silence. For minutes.

"Want to watch some Jeopardy?" Henry set down his carving and reached for the remote. The TV came to life before Joanna could respond. The show's theme song buzzed through the room. Should she come right out and ask? Was it his hesitancy about the adoption? Something else?

Joanna worked her needles. During the first commercial break, she spoke. "You feeling all right?"

"Fine. Just fine." Henry barely glanced away from the screen.

Joanna watched him. As the show returned he got two

right answers then cursed himself for getting a wrong one. Was she imagining it? Many times before she'd been sure something was wrong and he'd assured her it wasn't. Projecting, he'd say. Something was bothering her, not him. It could be true tonight ... but she didn't think so. "Would you like to go downtown this weekend? The flowers at the community garden should be in bloom. It'd be a nice walk."

Henry looked up. "I thought ... seeing all the families? You ready for that?"

"Normal life, right? That's what normal couples do. Kids or no kids."

Henry nodded. He smiled. "Sounds great."

As the show returned, he turned his gaze back to the screen. Four more questions and answers went by. He didn't answer a single one; he sat as if he didn't even hear them. Joanna kept her gaze on him. At last he looked up. "You're pretty connected to the idea of a newborn?"

"Yes." Joanna set the needles on her lap. "Are you? I thought we could discuss that with the psychologist, the possible difficulties going with babies up to two." Joanna hesitated. "And the possible benefits."

"That makes sense." Henry pulled his gaze away. He seemed to study the floor. The contestants on the screen continued their game. Clearly, Henry wasn't hearing a word of it. His head popped up. "What about older?"

"Older?"

"Older."

Joanna paused. "I'd never considered it. This was a way to get our baby. To—"

"But the real goal is to raise a child. To be parents. To grow our family."

"I suppose." Joanna set her knitting aside.

"And that's why you're suddenly open to adoption again. Because we want a family. We want to be parents."

"Yes."

"All those years ... I would have been open to adoption. I was open. But you weren't. You thought it erased hope. But adoption is a new kind of hope. A tangible hope. And giving hope, too, to a child who needs a family."

"Yes, but," Joanna shifted, "where is this coming from?"

Henry clasped and unclasped his hands. "One of the fellas on the new job. Joe. His wife works with family services or some such department. Can't remember the name of it. Said how she's so stressed. They're making changes. She's the administrator at this home for children."

Henry stopped. He swallowed. Nervous. Why was he so nervous?

"Some of the kids have parents who aren't able to take care of them right now. Others don't. Or their parents gave them up or ... well ... that used to be the case but they're changing things, see. From here on out they'll just have children who need temporary care—ones in and out of foster care or who need a place for a bit until they return home—until their parents get their lives together or they're placed with relatives or something." Henry stopped. Took a breath. "No kids who are eligible to be adopted anymore. Those kids will be sent elsewhere."

"Okay." Joanna swallowed.

"But only one kid like that is left. A little girl. A four year old." Henry tapped a foot and edged closer to Joanna. "Apparently she's been through a ton of upheaval, and Joe's wife, she's worried for her, scared what another move will do, if she'll get the attention she needs." Henry stopped again. He gave Joanna the slightest smile. An almost pleading smile. "This girl's going to be sent to the other side of the province. To an orphanage I guess you'd call it. His wife says once kids go to this particular one it's usually the end of the road for them."

"End of the—?"

"Well, I guess it's not horrible or anything, but it's the place children go when no one wants them." He shook his head. "Isn't that sad—that no one would want a child?"

Joanna nodded.

"Anyway, Joe says his wife says people almost never adopt older kids, especially kids who've been in and out of foster care and this one, this little girl—it's tearing the wife apart to think this girl will never get her family."

Joanna's chest tightened.

Henry sat straighter, his eyes bright. "I know it's not what we talked about. I know it's not part of the plan. But when Joe was talking about this he had no idea about our situation. None at all. And I just kept imagining this little girl with no one who wanted her. I started asking questions. Joe didn't know a whole lot but he said he'd try to get some basics from his wife."

"Henry?"

Henry kept on. "So today he came back with those basics. If things went well we could have this girl in weeks. There'd be no mother to take her away, to change her mind, the mother's long gone."

"What do you—"

"Dead. Abandoned the girl. I don't know. But she's not coming back."

Joanna's stomach twisted. Henry was right. This was not the plan. Not what she wanted. Her voice caught in her throat. "And you think we should adopt her?"

"I think ..." Henry leaned back against the couch. He clasped his hands on his lap. "I think this is a child in need of parents. And we're parents in need of a child. Or at least we could be."

Joanna rubbed a hand along her face. Breathed.

Henry's smile blossomed. "It seemed like a chance, you know? Or fate or something. This new worker happens to talk to me about this just days after we decide, after all these years, to be open to adoption? Maybe it means something."

Maybe it means something? Joanna kept her gaze on Henry, a frown on her face. How much was she supposed to give up? How much could one woman handle? She nodded slightly, not wanting Henry to see how much she wanted to scream, to cry, to yell at life! First the loss of all her babies, then the loss of even the dream of ever having her own baby, and now this, the loss of this new hope—to take a newborn into her arms and into her heart ... could a four year old ever really be her child? Doubtful.

"Joanna?" Henry leaned forward.

"I'm thinking." Joanna snapped. She adjusted her voice: soft, contemplative. "Based on things I've read and something Meverly mentioned—adopting an older child, it may lower our chances of getting a baby one day."

"But if the mother liked the idea of her child having a brother or sister, it could improve it."

Joanna nodded. It could ... only if the mother pushed. The agencies, the province, they'd push the mother in the direction of parents still waiting for a child—or at least that's the understanding Joanna had of the situation.

"Anyway." Henry stood and stepped toward Joanna. He bent low to kiss her forehead. "It's something we should explore. Something I want to explore." He straightened, a grin on his face, then turned off the TV. Joanna's brow furrowed. Henry's smile faded. "Just think on it." He squeezed her shoulder. "I'm off to take my shower."

Joanna nodded again. Thirteen years of marriage and at times Henry still seemed a mystery. Brooding all night ... well, not brooding exactly, but clearly nervous, hesitant of saying what was on his mind. And then he says it and suddenly everything is casual, back to normal. He'd walked away as if he'd asked Joanna nothing more than whether she wanted chicken or fish for dinner.

He'd always been casual about things. Those first few years of trying he'd said it would happen. He'd had complete confidence, or at least he seemed to. He'd had confidence in her too. When her 'time of the month' had her doubled over in pain, when the doctors told her some women didn't handle these things as well as others, when her mother affirmed their words, saying Joanna had always been delicate, Henry had said no. He'd insisted Joanna was strong. Insisted they keep looking for an answer to that pain, for an answer to why she lost another and yet another baby. Joanna being delicate was not an answer he would accept—that wasn't taking life casually. But he seemed casual about this.

Joanna picked up her knitting. She knit one, two, three stitches, then set it back down, remembering all the years of confusion, of feeling less. Exhaustion weighed on her for weeks sometimes. Getting out of bed seemed a challenge. But unless it was a day she physically couldn't, she always got out of bed. She always put on a smile when people came to the door. She even smiled when the doctors told her the pain was in her head. Henry didn't though. Henry asserted something was wrong. He believed, even when she found it hard to. When she got tired of constantly arguing the case of her own sanity, he argued for her. That's why they'd survived the years of pain, because he believed in her, because he wasn't casual about her—wasn't dismissive. Because he wanted her.

And now he wanted this little girl. Or, at least, wanted Joanna to be open to the possibility of her. If Joanna were healthy Henry would have a girl of his own by now, or a boy, maybe multiples. Five had been the number they'd talked about in those early years of marriage. Five. And they had made five babies. They'd never considered that they wouldn't hold a single one of them.

Joanna had offered a way out about nine years ago. After the third miscarriage. Told him he hadn't signed up for a sick wife. Said he should just leave. Find another woman. Make a family.

He'd gripped her, hard. Held on with a ferocity she'd never seen in him. But she hadn't been afraid. Looking into his eyes she'd been more in love than ever before. "Never say those words again," he spouted, his teeth gritted. "I want you. I married you."

That was the one and only time she suggested he leave.

Joanna walked to the bathroom. She stood outside the door and listened until the water stopped. She rapped on the door.

"Come in."

Henry stood with a towel around his waist. After all these years, the sight of him still made her blush. He was a beautiful man. Tall. Not broad exactly, but muscular. The body of a man who'd spent his whole life working.

"I'll be done in a second." He wore a half grin as he looked at her in the mirror. "Unless you want to hop back in there."

Another blush crept up Joanna's cheeks. She lifted a hand to her face. "No. Not that." She looked to the shower curtain. "Not tonight." Henry was the only man she'd ever been with. The only man she'd ever wanted. And he'd always been so tender. So patient. He'd given her so much. "You want to meet this girl?"

Henry dropped the hand that held a brush to his hair. "I do." He turned to Joanna. "I heard Joe talking about her and something inside me," his eyes lit, "a part of me that lay dormant, sprang to life." He stopped. "His wife called her a little angel. Maybe she'd be our miracle."

"Our miracle." Joanna stepped toward Henry but stopped a few feet away. She leaned against the wall. "He didn't say why no one wanted her? Why she was in and out of foster homes?"

"No."

"You didn't ask?"

"I didn't even tell him we were thinking of adoption. I thought I should talk to you first. But I can find out. I can ask."

"Maybe."

"Joe's wife wanted to take her, but they have four kids."

Joanna offered a smile. A four year old. Not a baby. A little person, with thoughts and habits and memories. Henry stepped toward Joanna. If he reached out, he could touch her, but he didn't. "It could mean no more waiting. Just think, waking up and making teddy bear pancakes. Visits to the park. Weekends camping, maybe."

"Me, camping?" Joanna laughed.

Henry chuckled. As the laugh petered out, so did his smile. "That adoption lady, she scared me, Jo. It seemed like the whole process could be so drawn out, full of hopes raised and dashed, again and again. We've had enough of that." Now he did reach out. His hand grasped hers. "I don't want to push, but I have to be honest ... the uncertainty of waiting on a baby we may never get—it's not something I look forward to. But this? This little girl could be our child. The child we've been waiting for."

Henry's eyes—scared but hopeful—broke her. Years of pain swam below the surface. That had been what first drew her to him, the pain. Carolyn had been adventurous. Daring. A risk-taker. Though six months pregnant, she'd accompanied her class on a post-graduation concert tour. On one stop, they'd helped a church congregation put up a new building after a fire. Carolyn took a fall when working to help put up the walls of the new chapel—a bad fall—and never recovered.

Joanna swallowed. She looked away from Henry, the memories coming back to her. Joanna had sat in the ambulance beside Carolyn on the way to the hospital. She'd been the one to tell Henry the news when he burst through the hospital doors to learn his wife was in surgery. And in the days and weeks afterwards, as Carolyn fought for life, Joanna had come to the hospital every day to visit her favourite teacher, and to hold the hand of the man that teacher loved. He was older than her, sure. Her friends thought it was weird. But she'd never seen a person love anyone that much. Never seen anyone hurt so bad. And she wanted to do all she could to take it away. She'd done the best she could. And then, in the weeks and months after Carolyn's death, Joanna had fallen in love.

She looked at Henry again. Henry, who'd had so much joy torn away but still found it within him to love her. Who now, despite it all, held onto hope once more. Who seemed excited. It had been her dream in those first months together to give him a new passion for life. To give him the love and the family he thought he'd lost with Carolyn's last breath. And she'd tried. Tried and tried. The least she could give him was this, a chance to meet the girl. Joanna squeezed out the words. "A visit. No commitment. No expectation?"

"Sure." Henry nodded. Smiled. "I don't even know if it's that simple, but if it is ... it has to be simpler than waiting in line for a child who's not even born yet. Most likely, not even conceived."

Joanna nodded. Maybe it would be simple. They could meet her. And once they did, if it didn't feel right, they could walk away.

CHAPTER NINE

Only five days after Henry had brought home the idea of the little girl in the group home, Joanna and he were driving toward the Nova Scotia Children and Youth Transition Centre. Joanna sat with her hands in her lap, tightly clasped. Joe's wife, Nancy her name was, had set things up quickly. When Joanna spoke with her on the phone she'd sounded eager, excited. Kind. She spoke with a rural Nova Scotian accent, the kind that Joanna always associated with a particularly trustworthy person. A solid person. Her nanny had had that accent.

Nancy assured Joanna a visit was no form of commitment. But it felt like commitment. She thought back to the moment she'd agreed to this visit, agreed in order to give Henry a chance at hope. In the past few days he'd let that hope grow. He stood taller, had a bounce to his step. Laughed a time or two as he told her to just imagine—a little girl running down their halls. *Do you think she'll have straight hair or curly?* He asked the night before last. *What if she doesn't like pancakes?*

He was definitely hopeful. And this trip, this visit, did it mean saying goodbye to ever holding a baby in her arms? What could be so wrong with this child that would make them say no, not her. Maybe if the child disliked them? How likely was that? They were nice people. Pleasant people. She glanced at Henry. If he saw this girl and wanted her, really wanted her, could Joanna say no? If she did because of hope of a baby and that baby never came, would he ever forgive her?

He wasn't thinking about the negatives. Yet for the past few days the negatives were all Joanna could see, the fact that maybe *no* child would be better than this child. A child who had a whole other life. Other parents. Who no one wanted.

Joanna could almost hear her mother's words—*a ragamuffin, a cast off.* Her breath felt stilted. A child who no one wanted? But those were her mother's words, her mother's thoughts. She was not her mother.

Joanna glanced at Henry again—his strong jaw, the hint of excitement etched along it. In many ways she was her mother: her obsession with cleaning, with things being 'just so'. Not in this way though. She wouldn't be her mother in this way. Marie had put all these negative, overcautious thoughts in Joanna's mind. The child wasn't a cast off. She was a child. A little girl in need of a home. Nothing more. Nothing less.

Henry pulled into the long driveway. It looked more like an oddly spaced row of townhouses than a home. Two buildings, each the width of two regular houses, sat beside each other with a walkway between them. Simple rectangles. No character. No aesthetic appeal. Joanna glanced at Henry.

Everything he made was beautiful. He'd talked about it multiple times, the importance of a home being somewhere a person could drive up to and love from the outside just as much as the inside.

She sat in her seat, waiting for him to come around and open her door. A silly habit, she knew. Impractical. But she enjoyed it anyway. He smiled down at her as she slipped her hand in his. Well, not completely impractical. The big truck he drove for work was a little tricky to get in and out of, especially in heels. He kept hold of her hand as they walked to the main door, far on the left hand side of the building.

Inside, the walls were an off white. Clean. As was the floor. But the walls were flat and bare. Henry and Joanna followed a sign to the main office. Henry tapped gently on the partially open door. A woman turned and smiled—an exhausted but welcoming smile. "Henry." She stepped forward, her hand outstretched. The voice was clearly Nancy's. "And you must be Joanna."

The woman's handshake was firm, businesslike, almost manly. "Nice to meet you, Nancy?"

"Yes, yes. Sorry. Look at me, dear, so eager I don't even introduce myself." She had a loud laugh. Raucous almost. Nancy stepped back to her desk, straightened a few items, then stepped out into the hall. Henry and she chatted casually about the number of children in residence, the number of staff, the upcoming changes. Joanna barely heard their words as she followed them through one set of doors and then another. They passed a row of rooms. Bright clothing was strewn across chair backs and hand painted works of art covered the walls.

Nancy pushed open the door at the end of the hall. "This

here is one of the activity rooms. The youngsters keep right busy."

Laughter reverberated off the walls. Joanna quickened her step to catch up to Nancy and Henry, only now realizing she'd lagged behind.

The room was full of children. And noise. Two boys sat at a train set, pushing the hand sized locomotives. Girls with ribbons in their hair stood before a kitchenette, mini saucepans and spatulas in hand. Older children sat at desks, presumably working on homework. One boy's tongue stuck out the side of his mouth in concentration. Others sat in front of a TV.

Joanna's gaze fell upon a girl in a corner. She was turned away from the rest and held a baby doll in her arms. She cradled the doll and murmured as she rocked it. As if sensing their presence, she turned. Her hair, the colour of wheat, glistened in the sunlight streaming through a nearby window. Her eyes were the colour of a Caribbean Ocean. Her skin, though tan, seemed moist and frail. This was the girl. Joanna could feel it. She'd be five soon—that's what Nancy had said—but she barely looked three. She was petite. Her limbs seemed like they could snap at the slightest force. The girl's eyes met Joanna's. They were wide, not exactly fearful, but wary, cautious. This was her. Joanna's heart constricted. This was love.

"Tracey." Nancy's voice held a smile. They were now only a step or two away from the girl. "This is Mr. And Mrs. Sampson. They've come to say hello to you."

The girl stood. Joanna swallowed. Fear, expectation, joy, swam over her. This was her daughter. This child was meant to be hers.

Henry bent to his knees. He was still almost a foot taller than the girl. He put out his hand. She hesitated before offering hers; it disappeared in his grasp. "Hello, Tracey."

"Hi." Her voice was as small as she was. A shiver ran through Joanna. She lowered down beside Henry.

"I'm Henry, and this is my wife, Joanna." Henry released the girl's hand.

Tracey nodded at them.

"Hi, Tracey."

The girl rocked on her heels. She offered the slightest smile. "I like your dress."

Joanna grinned. "Thank you. And you have just about the prettiest hair and eyes I've ever seen."

The girl's smile blossomed. Nancy leaned over them. "Perhaps you'd like to show Mr. And Mrs. Sampson what a great artist you are?"

Tracey nodded and headed toward an arts and crafts table on the other side of the room. She walked slowly and looked back every few steps as if to make sure the couple were still behind her. She sat and waited for Joanna and Henry to sit across from her. She reached for a piece of paper, a pack of crayons, bent her head down so low Joanna could only see one corner of the page, and got to work. Joanna and Henry looked at each other. This child meant business. Henry reached for Joanna's hand under the table. He squeezed.

A little less than ten minutes later Tracey sat up, turned the paper around and slid it over. It was them—Joanna and Henry. The girl had drawn Joanna's dress with the bright polka dots, her hair just cresting her shoulder. Henry's proportions were a little off. Joanna only reached a little above his waist instead of his upper chest. A rainbow spread through the sky above them and bright, albeit giant, flowers dotted the green grass on either side of them. "Do you like it?" Tracey's voice was almost inaudible.

"It's beautiful." Joanna lifted the paper to look more closely.

"You're an artist." said Henry.

Tracey grinned.

"Can we draw one together now?"

Tracey gave a little nod and Henry scooted around the small table to slide in beside the girl. "You like dinosaurs?" Tracey pressed her lips together and shook her head. "Tigers?" She nodded vehemently. Henry laughed. "All right then."

Henry got to work on a tiger. He lifted the page and made it roar. The girl jumped then giggled, both hands covering her mouth. She grabbed another page and drew a quick cow. She pointed to it. Henry let out a loud "Mooooo." More laughter. After another couple of drawings, the girl pushed the papers aside. She'd say an animal then Henry would make the noise, while coming up with a corresponding action. He bobbed his head for a rooster, danced on his toes with his arms held wide for a monkey, and crouched, pretending to lick his 'paw' when asked to be a cat. Within a minute or two almost all of the younger children crowded around him. Many of the older children turned to see what was going on, pretending not to be interested, though clearly captivated. Joanna stood next to Nancy, watching the scene.

"He's some good with kids." Nancy's laugh echoed off the walls. "A natural."

Joanna nodded.

"Your thoughts on Tracey?"

Joanna's throat clenched. All the nervousness and fear from earlier in the day flooded over her, but now for a different reason. "She's perfect."

Nancy glanced toward Joanna. "Mind you, she'll come with her trials. Any child who's gone through the abandonment and upheaval this one's had has scars." Nancy turned her gaze back toward Henry and the children. "But she's a gentle, kindhearted little soul. It's a sin what she's been through, and yet she's not angry like some. Withdrawn, but sweet as can be."

"Abandonment?" Joanna's gaze shifted away from Henry and the children. "What—"

Nancy patted Joanna's arm. "How about we wait to talk about that until Henry's with us?"

Joanna turned her gaze back to Henry and the children. She wrapped her arms around her middle. How could *anyone* abandon this little girl?

CHAPTER TEN

Several minutes later, after Henry had run out of his arsenal of animal noises and Joanna had spent a few minutes letting Tracey show her her favourite toys, Henry and Joanna sat in Nancy's office.

"I think you've made a friend." Nancy grinned. "The girl was glowing."

Henry's eyes and voice were full of excitement. "She's delightful."

Nancy folded her arms on the desk. Her face turned business. "Tracey's been in our care a long time. In and out of foster homes, but still under our care, for over two years."

Henry leaned forward. "Is that abnormal?"

"For older children, no. Sadly, it's not. For a child who came to us as young as Tracey, it's certainly not normal."

"Well, why ..." Joanna's voice trailed off.

"The poor sweet thing, she arrived sick as a dog. Bless her

heart, she's spent almost four months of those two years in and out of hospital. She's a weak little girl. Constitution-wise, I mean. From what we understand, that's the reason her mother relinquished parenting rights."

"She just—"

Joanna cut Henry off. "She gave away her child because she was sick? What kind of—"

Nancy raised a hand. "There's no need for judgement here. Her mother did what she felt was right. I got the impression from Tracey's original caseworker that the mother was young and unsupported." Nancy leaned forward. "If she didn't believe she could be the parent Tracey needed, she did the right thing placing her for adoption. And she didn't cast her away, she arranged an adoptive family for her. A young couple who'd been trying for years. But there was an accident and the wife was badly injured." Nancy looked away, as if remembering. "She needed round the clock care. It would have been too much, taking on Tracey, who needed a lot of care as well. They had her for less than a week when the accident happened." Nancy put a hand to her head. "A fine kettle of fish." She paused. "Horrible." She looked to the desk a moment, seeming to fight back the memories. "I don't know if Tracey even remembers. She cried and cried." Nancy shook her head and exhaled. "It must have been confusing. Traumatic. Shuffled from place to place—here for a week, there for a week, then back here—not knowing or understanding where her mom was and why she left." Nancy's voice caught. She coughed and straightened her shoulders. "It was a closed adoption so the birth mother doesn't know Tracey didn't stay with that family. Doesn't know she's been here these past years."

"That doesn't seem right." Henry leaned forward. "What if the mother would have wanted her back?"

Nancy shrugged. "I don't make the rules."

Joanna rubbed a hand along her arm. "What? I mean," she glanced to Henry, "she doesn't seem sick."

Nancy brightened. "The lass has actually been doing amazingly well the past few months. She's getting some strength. She's gaining weight. A little miracle. The doctors don't know what was causing her illnesses. They ran countless tests. It didn't seem to be any one thing." Nancy waved her hand. "She'd get the flu, then right after an unending cold, ear infections, symptoms that seemed like food poisoning when all of the other children—eating all the same things—were fine." Nancy paused. "They figured an underdeveloped or compromised immune system. As you can imagine, our constant rotation of other children did not help her situation. Little germ carriers, they all are. We tried placing her in foster homes without many kids but germs are everywhere I guess, and most foster parents don't sign up to take care of a perpetually sick child."

Henry rubbed his chin. He looked at Joanna, his brow furrowed and his jaw tense. "So she was quite sick then. She required a lot of care."

"But Nancy said she's better now." Joanna turned her gaze to Nancy. "Right?"

"She's been doing better." Nancy nodded. "A sensitive child, that one. Forms strong attachments. Staff or other children leaving seem to trigger these balls of stress in her, which generally triggers another round of illness. This is a little girl in want of a family. A stable family. The one good thing about the orphanage would be some stability." Nancy folded her hands. "But staff would still change. Occasionally, children would get adopted or transferred." Nancy spread her hands across the desk. "It's always better for a child to be in a loving family. To have a home. Some place they know is theirs."

"We could give her that." Joanna turned her head toward Henry then snapped it back to Nancy. "I'm a homemaker, primarily, although I do the books for Henry's business. But I do that from home and if he needed to hire an assistant because Tracey needed my care, he could do that. He's done it in the past when I was ..." Joanna hesitated. She couldn't tell this woman about her bouts of pain, the days after yet another miscarriage or surgery when she found it hard to get out of bed. "When I was especially busy."

"Sweetie." Henry rested a hand on her leg, his tone altered from just minutes before. "Don't rush ahead. We just came here to meet Tracey, to—"

"To be open to the possibility." Joanna could hear the desperation in her voice. "I'm open. We've met her and ..." she paused, "It could work. I think ... well, it could."

Nancy glanced between Henry and Joanna. "You two ought to take some time to discuss this. You've already contacted the adoption agency?" Joanna nodded. "Had your assessments yet?"

"Home assessment, not psychological," said Henry.

"It's scheduled for late next week."

"That's good." Nancy looked to the papers on her desk, just to look away from them it seemed. She looked back up. "I'm glad you two have interest in Tracey. Not many people want to adopt an older child." Nancy's gaze shifted to Henry. "And Joe says you're good people." She let it drift toward

Joanna. "You seem it."

Henry let out a puff of air. "Level with me here, Nancy. How sick is she? Could she," he coughed, a forced one, "could she die, or … I mean …"

Joanna's throat tightened. Surely, no. It was ridiculous for him to even ask. The child was tiny, frail looking, but—

"She came close a few times." Nancy bit her lip. "Terrible stuff." She templed her fingers. "But she always bounced back. She's a fighter, that one. And as I said, she's doing well of late. Best I've seen her."

"But for all you know it could happen again?" Henry pushed.

Nancy nodded. "For all we know, yes."

Joanna sat straight in the chair but the room wavered. Tracey could die. Joanna could take that sweet little girl home, tuck her in at night, braid her hair, cuddle her on the couch—and then she could die? Another child gone. A weight lay across Joanna's chest. Only when Henry's fingers travelled from her leg to her hand did she realize it was trembling. Their eyes met. Even if she could handle this— losing another child—could he?

Nancy pushed her chair back as if to stand but stayed seated. "The transition is happening in three weeks. That's not much time. And you don't need to make your decision before then, but if you did we'd do our best to have her with you before the transfer." Nancy shifted forward. "It'd be tight, but the system can move quickly when needed. If you decide you want Tracey, if everything works out for you to take her, it would be a much smoother transition if she went directly from here to you." Nancy stood. "Take as long as you need. When you decide, if your decision is to pursue adoption, we'll start the process."

Joanna popped out of her chair. "Give us a few minutes? Just ..." She looked to Henry then back to Nancy, her pulse racing. "Excuse us for a few minutes?"

Nancy smiled, a hesitant look on her face, walked past them, and closed the office door.

"Jo?"

Joanna sank back into her chair and swivelled toward Henry. "Let's do this."

"Jo—"

"You don't want to?"

He shook his head. "It's not that. Not exactly."

"She's a sweet girl."

"She is." He smiled. "A darling girl. But she's sick, Jo."

Joanna shrugged. "I'm sick. And you still want me."

Henry let out a half laugh.

"Besides, she's not sick anymore. She's been doing better."

He nodded. "But what if that changed? What if—"

"It's terrifying." Joanna reached for Henry's hand. "We've already lost so much." Joanna stopped, her gaze locking with his. "But it's like you said, this is a child in need of a parent. Desperately in need. And we're parents waiting for their child. Parents who could give her love and stability."

Henry's shoulders sank. "Could you handle it? If something happened to her, if ..."

Joanna looked to their hands, still clasped. "We've handled everything else." She brought her gaze back up. "What about you? Could you—"

Henry held his lips tight. He looked away from her. Was he thinking of Carolyn. Of their child. Of all the other unborn babies through the years? Wondering what it would be like to watch another person he loved die?

That was an experience he had that Joanna did not. Not that Joanna hadn't loved Carolyn too ... she had. That's why she'd visited her former teacher's hospital bed so often in those final weeks. But it wasn't the same thing. She couldn't compare it. Losing a teacher and mentor was nothing compared to losing your wife. Joanna shuddered at the memory, the way Henry had sat by Carolyn's bedside night and day. The look of sadness, defeat, as he watched her grow weaker and weaker, as she struggled to survive. And all the while knowing their baby—who couldn't be taken out due to the stress and risk either surgery or induced labour would cause Carolyn—struggled along with her.

And then the moment she'd stopped struggling. They'd tried to save the baby, but it was too late. Joanna arrived just minutes after the emergency C-section. Henry turned to look at her, misery like Joanna had never encountered throbbing from him. When the doctor finally convinced him to leave Carolyn's side, he clung to Joanna. Held her like she was oxygen and he was a drowning man.

She still couldn't fathom what that moment must have felt like to him. Did it compare to her own losses? She couldn't know.

But Henry had those losses too, had watched Joanna as she clung to life when one of the miscarriages had come close to killing her. And then her surgery, which, arguably, had come even closer.

Joanna reached for Henry's hand. He raised his head. "It's you I'm worried about. You're the one who'd be home with her all the time, watching. I know what that's like." He shook his head. "It almost ruined me." A long pause. "But she's not that sick right now ... may never be again. That's a reason to hope."

Joanna squeezed his hand, heart aching for the fact that he was remembering, that after all these years she could still see the pain in his eyes—so fresh. "I can handle it." She smiled at him. "A tangible hope, right? Sick or not. She'd be our child."

Henry chuckled. "Tangible indeed. She's right down the hall."

Let's do this." Joanna grasped Henry's other hand.

"It could mean never having a baby."

Joanna nodded. "That was my thought from the moment you mentioned this, but the second I saw her—" Joanna stopped. "She's meant to be ours." Her eyes glistened and her smile grew. "It stopped being about what I wanted. It was about what she needed. What we could give."

Henry's grasp tightened around her fingers. "My thoughts exactly."

CHAPTER ELEVEN

Henry and Joanna left the group home with nervous smiles on their faces. Joanna's stomach flipped and flopped. Good flips-flops though, excited ones. Nancy hadn't been as pleased as Joanna had hoped. Hesitant was a better word. She'd encouraged Joanna and Henry to go home and think about their decision for a few days, emphasized this was a huge decision, to take a child into their home, a child who could get sick again.

Any child could get sick though, Joanna interjected. Nancy had nodded. Offered a tight-lipped smile. She told them not a word of it would be spoken to Tracey until everything had been lined up—every form processed, every dotted line signed. They all agreed they'd do what they could to speed the process. Henry and Joanna had left Nancy's office with instructions to call Meverly tomorrow, let her know of their change in status, see if they could get their psych assessment moved sooner. If not, Nancy assured them, the end of the week should still be doable so long as they got the paperwork in place.

Later that day, when she walked through their front door, Joanna didn't step into their home, but a place full of possibility. She'd always imagined bringing a baby through that door, but in just a few weeks, if everything went well—and it had to go well—they'd be bringing a four-year-old. "We'll have to get a bed and a dresser and toys. Books. Everything we have is for a newborn." Joanna turned to Henry. "What size do you think she wears? Or her favourite books? She showed us the toys she liked, but what about books?"

Henry pulled Joanna against his chest. "We'll figure it out. Besides," a laugh entered his voice, "she'll come with clothes."

"But—"

"Tonight," he gave her a squeeze, "let's rest. Tomorrow you can go mad with planning." Joanna wanted to protest. Henry grinned. "Deal?"

Joanna nodded and sank into his arms. "You hungry?"

"Starved."

"Spaghetti and meat sauce?"

"Perfect."

The next morning, after seeing Henry off for the day, Joanna picked up the phone to call Meverly. She froze with it just inches from her ear. Everything needed to go as smoothly as possible. An in person meeting would make that more likely. Joanna grabbed the keys for her car, knowing she could drive into the city just to learn Meverly would be out on a home visit or simply not free to see her. But if that were the case a call wouldn't work either. She'd take her chances.

Joanna double checked the address for the adoption agency before stepping out of her car. She stood in front of a small, squat, nondescript building. The agency must be one of the units inside. After looking at the list of offices, Joanna made her way up a set of concrete steps and to the correct unit. She'd expected glass panelled walls, but only a solid door greeted her. She knocked. Nothing. Another knock. She counted to thirty then took hold of the handle. The waiting room was as small and nondescript as the building—minus the photos on the wall, so densely plastered she couldn't see the paint in most places. Parents and children. Babies certainly dominated the pictures, but older children adorned the wall too. And every photo looked happy. Every photo looked like a family. Joanna's heart swelled. In a few weeks their photo could be on that wall. Her, Henry, and Tracey. A family.

The waiting room held six chairs, a small area with toys that looked as old as she, another door in the far corner, and a small desk—unoccupied. On the desk sat one of those little metal bells. If no one had heard her knocking, certainly the bell would do no good. Still, Joanna pinged it.

Foolish, to come instead of call. At least if she'd called she could have left a message. What would she do here, scrawl a note on a piece of paper and leave it on the desk?

Joanna waited, pinged the bell once more. As she was about to leave, a sound to her left stopped her. The door in the corner opened, revealing Meverly.

"Mrs. Sampson?"

"Hi, hello!" Joanna glided toward Meverly and put out her hand.

"Is everything all right?"

"Wonderful."

Meverly dropped Joanna's hand. "I hope you weren't waiting long. My receptionist is ill and I was on a call." Meverly glanced at her watch. "Did we have an appointment?"

"Oh, no." Joanna stepped back. "I just wanted to talk to you and I ... well, I was coming to town anyway so I thought I'd pop in and see if you were available." Joanna gave her most winning smile. "Do you have a few minutes?"

Meverly looked at her watch again. "A few. Then I have to leave."

"Great." Joanna followed Meverly into her office. It had a fresh coat of paint and looked much more inviting than the waiting room. Here, too, framed photos lined the walls.

"What can I do for you?" Meverly sat behind a desk and motioned for Joanna to sit in the chair across from it.

"Henry and I have decided to adopt a little girl named Tracey. She's four years old."

Meverly's brow raised. "Tracey Dunnett?"

"I didn't get her last name."

"She's at the Nova Scotia Children and Youth Transition Centre?"

"Yes."

Meverly tapped her pen against her desk. "How did this happen? I thought you were only open to infants."

"Fate, perhaps." Joanna explained how Henry had learned about the situation from his employee. "Something sparked in my husband and it went from there. We met her yesterday."

"Tracey or Nancy?"

"Both."

"And you ..."

"We want to adopt her."

Meverly inhaled deeply. "Mrs. Sampson, I spoke to you less than two weeks ago. You were adamant about adopting an infant. So adamant in fact you didn't want to even consider a toddler. Now you're willing to take ... how old is Tracey?"

"Four. Almost five."

"You can see why this is surprising."

Joanna looked to her lap. She could see it. Sure she could see it. She raised her gaze to Meverly. "When Henry came home with this idea it scared me. I was against it. I won't lie to you. I wanted a baby. I've always wanted a baby. But I told him I would be open. I would meet her. And when I did ..." A smile stretched across Joanna's face. "I'm certain she's meant to be with us. I'd always imagined what it would feel like to be a mother, to look into my child's face for the first time. And looking at Tracey, I can't imagine that feeling would be much different."

Meverly visually softened, but only for a moment. "I need you to be aware, if this works out it could greatly lower your chances of adopting a newborn."

Joanna crossed her legs and sat taller. "You said our chances weren't great anyway."

"They aren't. But this could lower them."

"That's okay."

Meverly raised her brow again.

"Really." Confidence seeped through Joanna. "It's okay."

Meverly stood and went to a filing cabinet in the corner. "You're aware of the upcoming move. Would you like to to try to make this happen before then?"

"Absolutely."

Meverly, with energy to her step, brought a file back to the desk. "It'll be tough. But I've seen it happen."

CHAPTER TWELVE

Over the next few days Joanna felt trapped in a whirlwind. Papers to be filed and sent and signed, meetings to be had, and the psych assessment. They'd been told to block out the whole afternoon for the appointment. Joanna assumed the psychologist wasn't great at keeping to a schedule. Wrong. Their appointment lasted almost five hours. Two for Henry. Two for her. An hour together.

Dr. Johnson stared at Joanna then looked away. Stared. Scribbled. Looked away. His thick brows furrowed every time he wrote a note. His questions were invasive. Insulting. Almost accusatory at times. Joanna felt as if she were standing in front of him, naked. She came close to trembling as she took in his piercing looks, and gruff tone that accompanied question after question, all while scribbling on that legal-sized notepad.

After a two hour break, she re-entered the office to join

Henry. She shifted close and held his hand. When it seemed the appointment was drawing to a close, Henry leaned forward. "Level with us, Doc. Are you seeing any red flags?"

Dr. Johnson looked pointedly toward Joanna. "I'll put my findings in a report and send it to both the Children's Home and the provincial adoption agency."

"Is there nothing you can tell us?"

He uncrossed then recrossed his legs. "The speed of your decision concerns me, though I recognize in this case another move could be harmful for the child's mental health." Dr. Johnson looked to Joanna again and then back to Henry. "And your wife's condition concerns me. Based on her medical history, she's a weak woman. A woman who, having suffered the losses she has, may not be in the best position to care for a child."

Henry leaned forward. "Now just wait a min—"

The doctor raised his hand. "I see the notes from her medical doctors. Years of complaining about intense periods." He looked to Joanna. "Every woman gets periods. Notes that she doesn't seem able to handle the natural pain of being a woman, and all her miscarriages. It doesn't give a great impression. In fact, I've treated women like her before. Attention seekers. And a child like Tracey may need a lot of support, someone to really take care of her. It seems, Mr. Sampson, that your wife also needs taking care of."

Joanna froze in her chair. Yet another doctor talking about her as if she wasn't there. Yet another man proclaiming she was weak.

Henry scooted his chair closer to the doctor. "If you looked at those notes of yours you would see that Joanna has a disease—endometriosis. A disease which caused all that 'phantom pain' those incompetent doctors insisted she had. A disease which led to the miscarriages. And Joanna has powered through all of it. She's not weak. She's the strongest person I know.

Dr. Johnson glanced to his notes." I saw the word. I'm not familiar with-"

"Well, get familiar." Henry stood, pulling Joanna up along with him. "I see those fancy degrees up on your wall but maybe you need to do some more research. Educate yourself."

"Henry." Joanna laid her hand on his shoulder. This doctor could decide their fate. She put on a smile. She knew how to defend herself, but making this man angry would do no good.

The doctor remained seated. He looked to his notes again. "The disease caused the cysts? The need for surgery? I don't see how that explains the other symptoms."

"It explains all of it!" Henry leaned in.

"Disease or no disease. Justified illness or not, the point remains clear that Joanna's medical history is of concern. It is my responsibility to ensure this child goes to a home with people who can properly take care of her, especially considering her illness. What if your wife and the girl were sick at the same time?"

"Then I would take off work to take care of them both—if needed. Joanna goes about her days in more pain than most people could handle. Than you could handle. Besides, we have support. Our families. Our friends. If we'd had our own baby would you take it away because Joanna gets bad days?"

"Not unless we could prove the child was neglected."

"Henry." Joanna pulled on his arm once more. Her throat tightened. Her stomach twisted. The dream of Tracey was being yanked away.

"Outside of the medical records, did you see any reason why Joanna would not be an excellent mother?"

"Well ..."

"Spit it out."

Joanna let out a gasp. Henry's muscles tensed. His arm shook. Not that she thought he'd hit the man. He wouldn't, but ... she glanced toward the doctor. He was clearly wondering the same thing.

"She seems very reliant on this working out. Almost desperately so. That could be a red flag."

"Desperately wanting a child is a red flag? Would you prefer parents who didn't care? Who were casual about the outcome?"

"No, but—"

"This is ridiculous."

At last, Dr. Johnson stood. He seemed dwarfed in front of Henry. "Your behaviour, Mr. Sampson, is not helping matters."

Henry's shoulders drooped, his whole demeanour deflated like an old balloon. "Dr. Johnson, I mean no disrespect." He wrapped his arm around Joanna's shoulder. "You do not know my wife. You're looking at words on a page. Words written by men who didn't know or understand my wife's disease, what it could do to a woman. But I know." He looked to Joanna and squeezed her shoulder. "And I know it won't prevent her from being the most amazing mother in the world. All anyone can do is their best, and Joanna would do that." He turned his gaze back to the doctor. "I assure you, her best would be good enough. Better than that. And I'd do my best. Better than hundreds of parents who don't have to jump through the hoops we've been soaring through the past weeks, ones who become parents without even trying."

The doctor cleared his throat. "You can't expect us to just give children over to everyone."

Henry shook his head. "No. No I can't."

"And your temper concerns me."

"This isn't temper." Henry let out one of his most disarming grins. "This is adamant belief." He paused. "Are you married, Dr. Johnson?"

"I am."

"And would you not defend your wife?"

Dr. Johnson brought his arm up with an exaggerated motion and looked at his watch. "Our time has run out Mr. And Mrs. Sampson. I will prepare my report and pass it along." He cleared his throat. "You will have the opportunity to contest any of my findings should you so desire and book an appointment with an alternative psychologist."

Henry shook his head. Joanna, fear twisting at the core of her, thanked the doctor and led Henry out of the office. As soon as the door closed she turned toward Henry. Their arms wrapped around each other. "It'll be okay," Joanna whispered. "This man isn't the last word."

"No." Henry squeezed her tighter.

"And he only said he had reservations." Joanna pulled back and tilted her head to look at her husband. "You're my hero. You know that?"

Henry let out a chuckle, his eyes moist. "It wouldn't be right. It just wouldn't—"

"Shh." Joanna put her head against his chest, holding back threatened tears. "We'll figure it out"

CHAPTER THIRTEEN

Two days later, Joanna stood cleaning the breakfast dishes when the phone rang. She dried her hands, folded the dish cloth she'd been using, and walked to the phone. "Sampson residence. Joanna speaking."

The voice on the other end of the line was tense. "Joanna, this is Nancy. The assessment from the psychologist came in."

Joanna stood straighter. "It's not good?"

"Unfortunately not."

Joanna closed her eyes. She kept her voice even. "Tell me, please."

Nancy sighed. "The psychologist brought up your medical history. Your issues with conception, miscarriage, a lifetime of pain complaints when nothing seemed wrong with you." Nancy paused. "He recommends further rounds of assessment plus an additional home visit. He suggests a child with Tracey's history needs an extremely stable home and questioned your stability."

In the silence, Joanna waited for more. It didn't come. "Did he mention anything about Henry?"

Nancy paused, as if rifling through papers. "Just that he seemed to have a stable job, be a good provider. He commented that as Henry worked long hours you would be the primary caregiver. He seemed concerned with how you would handle that," Nancy paused again, "given your past physical and mental health."

"The pain wasn't in my head." Joanna gritted her teeth. "That's been proven. I wasn't weak. I wasn't just in need of attention."

More silence. "I see that. Your disease, I don't know much about it but," another pause, "would it make it hard for you to take care of Tracey, especially if she got sick again?"

"No."

"Okay." Nancy let out her breath with a whoosh.

"Is it over?" Joanna asked before Nancy could continue. "Is it too late? Is there—"

"No. No. Not at all." Nancy hurried to respond. "He suggested several weeks more of in depth assessments. That's better than saying ... well, it's better."

Joanna moved through the kitchen and pulled out a dining room chair. "That would mean there's no way we could adopt Tracey before she's sent to the orphanage."

"It's not likely."

Joanna closed her eyes again. She imagined that little girl— the girl she felt was meant to be her daughter—being moved again, sent to a new place, hours away, where she knew no one. She'd be confused. Scared. She'd think she was being sent because no one wanted her. "Is there anything else we can do?"

"If you had another assessment performed, soon, with another doctor, and if the report refuted Dr. Johnson's recommendations, there'd be a chance. If, however, the psychologist corroborated his report, it wouldn't look good."

Again, it didn't sound like Nancy was done speaking—though it didn't really sound like Nancy speaking at all, her easy colloquialisms gone. Joanna waited. "And?"

"And rushing the assessment could spark warning flags for a psychologist. Sometimes parents get obsessed with the idea of getting a child right away. Their motivation becomes about their needs, their desire to become parents, rather than about what's best for the child." She stopped, hesitated. "You wouldn't want to give that impression."

Was that the situation? Was she so eager to be a mother she cared more about fulfilling her needs and wants than about what was best for Tracey? Joanna stared out the window, searching herself. *Was it?* No. Absolutely not. She wanted to be a mother, yes. She'd always wanted to be a mother. But that dream was about holding her own baby in her arms. It was about nursing a child who'd come from her and Henry, teaching that baby to talk, to walk—seeing it grow. Maybe that dream was selfish, was about her needs, but this one wasn't. Adopting Tracey wasn't about what she wanted nearly as much as it was about what Tracey needed—love and support that Joanna could give. A home, consistency. Would it make her a mother? Yes. But more importantly, it would give Tracey a family.

Joanna's voice came out soft and strong. "I've been waiting for over thirteen years. I've been through more in my efforts to become a mother than most could handle. I'm not in any rush. A few extra weeks, a few extra months, that's nothing.

"The rush was for Tracey's sake. To make the transition easier for her. I want to mother this child. I love her already. And what that means is that if I won't be the best mother for her then I shouldn't be her mother at all." Joanna smiled into the receiver. "We'll do the second assessment. We'll wait as long as it takes. I know myself. I know that doctor was wrong. A second assessment will show that. I'm not perfect, not by any means, but that doesn't mean I can't be a great mother to Tracey. Just as good a mother as any other woman. I'm certain of that."

Nancy's laugh burst through the phone as the easy tone in her voice returned. "Exactly the answer I was hoping for. Listen, Joanna, I've been working this gig for a long time and I know how to read people. Like I said before, you and Henry are good people. I've also interacted with this Dr. Johnson before. I would never say he's a chauvinist, sexist pig," the laugh, "but I wouldn't contradict anyone who did, and more than one client has!" Nancy let out a sigh. "Any woman who's been through what you've been through has got to be strong. That's the truth. And one hundred percent, the rush is for Tracey, not you. That move to the orphanage—going all by herself—it'll terrify and confuse the darling. She'd adjust, of course, but not without damage done. To give that girl any more upheaval than necessary would be a sin."

More sounds of shuffling paper. "Okay, I know a psychologist who often does work with the center—assesses parents hoping to regain custody of their children, etc. She's a friend and a helluva woman. I bet I can get her to squeeze you in tomorrow. Can you make yourself free whatever time she is?"

"Yes." Joanna spewed the word, then regained her exposure. "Yes, of course."

"Great. I'll work like a dog if I have to to set that up and then, so long as she disputes every thing that Dr. Johnson said, I'll keep working to get this all done quick as a wink." Nancy let out a huff, as if she were already working hard. "You'll need a second home assessment." More shuffles. "Your criminal record checks came in. All spick and span there."

"Well, yes—"

"So, the tricky part will be getting a judge to approve Dr. Cavell's report over Dr. Johnson's. To get a rush on that. Honestly, dealing with the courts is often like threading a camel through the eye of a needle." Nancy chuckled. "I'm mixing my metaphors but you know what I mean." Another pause. "You're not best friends with a judge, are you?"

"No." Joanna rubbed a hand along her forearm. But her father was.

"We'll figure it out. We'll do our best. Maybe we can even buy some more time. If the gate keepers know a suitable family wants to adopt Tracey, they may extend her transition date."

"Oh," Joanna perked up, "that sounds like a great solution." She cleared her throat. "To save more time at least."

Nancy groaned. "It does seem like it. But it's not just Tracey who's being moved. See, we have about seven extra beds and another home out of town is moving all their wards over to us. As of yesterday they have eight children."

"So, if they still have eight at the time of the transition ..."

"Tracey has no where to go but the orphanage."

"I see." Silence lingered on the line.

"Chin up, all right? We'll do the best we can. When I'm on a mission I can bend, twist and break the rules like the best of them."

Joanna nodded then realized her goof. "That's great. Thank you, Nancy. I appreciate your support."

Again, that smile in her voice. "Joanna. Thank you. I'd been walking into the office every morning just hoping each day would be the day Tracey found her family. I love that child. I'd take her if I could."

"Joe said."

"Well, we can't. And I knew she'd need special people. People who wouldn't step away with fear when they learned they'd have a child battling sickness." Something dropped and Nancy mumbled under her breath, then spoke clearly. "You ask me, the fact that you and Henry know what that's like, that you've battled it yourself, makes you an even better match for Tracey. And if anyone does ask me, I'll tell them just that."

CHAPTER FOURTEEN

Joanna sat in Dr. Cavell's waiting room. The woman smiled when Joanna entered her office. She held out a manicured hand. She was young. Two, three years older than Joanna—at the most. She could be younger.

After introductions, Dr. Cavell motioned for Joanna to sit and offered that warm smile once more. "You must be nervous."

"No, I mean—"

"It's intimidating, to have someone assess your mental state. To say you're lacking in some way, and then to have to come in and succumb yourself to another assessment. It's enough to make anyone nervous. I would be."

Joanna chuckled. She exhaled, letting her shoulders relax slightly. "Yes, I guess I'm a little nervous."

"I understand." Dr. Cavell leaned forward. Unlike in Dr. Johnson's office, there was no desk separating them. "Rest assured that I will be basing my assessment one hundred percent on my own observations and findings. I didn't even look at Dr. Johnson's report as I don't want to be influenced in any way by what he had to say."

"So, you don't know?" Joanna smoothed a hand along her hair. "But you know why I'm here."

"I know you're looking to adopt a child. I know something in Dr. Johnson's report raised some red flags. I know Nancy asked me to squeeze you in, which means she's rooting for you. That's all I know."

Joanna nodded. "Okay."

"So should we begin?"

Another nod. Joanna relaxed more and more as the minutes ticked by. This appointment seemed more of a conversation than an assessment. Unlike Dr. Johnson, who'd interrogated her, Dr. Cavell simply asked questions, listened, and contributed her thoughts and opinions from time to time. She hardly wrote at all.

At the end of the hour Joanna stood in sync with Dr. Cavell. "How'd I do?" she asked, the nervous twinge returning to her voice.

Dr. Cavell put a hand to Joanna's shoulder. "I'm not supposed to say anything about your assessment. Speaking woman to woman, however, Dr. Johnson doesn't know the first thing about what it is to be a woman or what we can handle."

Joanna smiled. It wasn't an answer, exactly, but it was enough.

Rather than wait the thirty minutes it would take to get home, Joanna found a pay phone outside Dr. Cavell's office and stepped into the booth. "Henry?"

"Is everything all—"

"It's okay." Joanna closed her eyes as relief and happiness spilled over her.

"The doctor said?"

"Not exactly, but I can just feel it ... she'll refute Dr. Johnson's assessment. We'll still need a judge to approve hers, but," Joanna closed her eyes, "it's going to be okay."

Henry's laugh carried through the line. "I wasn't worried for a minute."

Joanna held the phone to her ear. She let the silence settle. "This may happen."

"I know." His voice sounded as incredulous as hers. "What's next?"

Joanna leaned against the glass wall of the booth, not even caring who may have been against it last. "We wait for the assessment and then we hope Nancy can push it through."

Joanna must have looked at the clock two dozen times the next morning. Each time wondering how long it would be before Nancy called. Finally, at 11:25, the phone rang.

"Hello?"

"Sweetie, is that how I taught you to answer the phone?"

Joanna's excitement waned. "Mother, hello. I was just waiting for a call."

"What does that have to do with it?"

Joanna pulled out a quick lie. "I thought it would be Henry. He doesn't need to know it's the Sampson residence."

"Well, it wasn't Henry, was it?"

Joanna bit her lip, a habit her mother would call her out on if she were here. "How are you doing today, Mother?"

"Not too well, actually."

Joanna tried not to roll her eyes. "What's wrong?" Joanna infused her voice with what she hoped sounded like curiosity and concern.

"This whole adoption thing you were going on about."

"It's not a thing."

"I've been trying to keep my feelings to myself, trying to remember you're a grown woman, but I can't keep silent. I don't like this, Joanna, not one bit."

Joanna looked to the ceiling. "It's not about whether you like it."

"Well, it should be. We've supported you all these years."

"Supported? Henry and I have never asked for—"

"But we've given, my dear. And you accepted."

"Presents."

"Generous presents. And some of those contracts your husband has gotten, big contracts of our friends and our friends' friends. You don't think he would have come across those on his own?"

"Mother."

"It would be an embarrassment—to take in some unwanted baby."

Joanna's chest tightened. "An embarrassment to whom?"

"To me, of course, to your father. And it should be to you too."

Joanna looked at the clock again. She could be missing Nancy's call. Nancy would call back, of course, but ... "This really isn't the best time, Mother. I should get going."

"What do you have to do?"

"I told you. I'm waiting for a call."

"From your husband. Is his call more important than

mine?"

Caught in her lie, Joanna contemplated what to say.

"Joanna, are you there?"

"I'm here."

"We need to talk about this."

"We don't."

"We do. What if the child has some horrible disease or her mother," a faint shudder travelled through the line, "what if the baby's born addicted to drugs? I read—"

"We're not adopting a baby."

"Well, thank goodness." Her mother let out a relieved laugh. "I don't know why you didn't just say—"

"We're adopting a four year old. Her name is Tracey, and I'm waiting for a call from the group home. I don't want to miss it."

"Joanna."

"I'll talk to you later." Joanna put down the phone. Her arm shook. Only once before had she ever hung up on her mother. She'd been at a friend's house, calling to tell her mother she was marrying Henry no matter what she or Joanna's father had to say. Marie arrived at the friend's house minutes later, ready to—quietly of course, without much outward fuss for neighbours to talk of—drag Joanna back home. But Joanna hadn't changed her mind that day, and she wouldn't today either.

CHAPTER FIFTEEN

Joanna expected she had between seventeen and nineteen minutes until her mother showed up at her doorstep. Fourteen if Marie pushed the speed limit.

Joanna set a kettle on the stove to boil. If her mother was coming, Joanna might as well be hospitable. As her mother had taught her, it was easier to express resolve with a cup of tea in your hand. If you looked composed, your opponent would seem ridiculous as she ranted and raved. Joanna just hoped Nancy's call didn't come when her mother was here, or even worse, just before. She could imagine her mother, in a rare moment of lost composure, hollering in the background for Nancy to hear. Joanna shuddered. She couldn't have that. If the call came, she'd simply give an excuse to get off the line when her mother's car pulled into the driveway. And if her mother was ranting when the phone rang? Joanna wouldn't answer.

Sixteen minutes later Marie's Cadillac pulled into the driveway. She'd probably pushed the speed limit a bit, but not much. Hopefully that meant she would still have some level of reserve.

Joanna stood at the door waiting. She pulled it open just as her mother's manicured hand was poised to knock. "Good morning."

"You expected I'd come?"

Joanna stood tall. She'd watched her mother ream out enough people over the years that she knew all the moves. She also knew how to counter them. She kept the image of Tracey looking back at her—those wide slightly fearful eyes— in the forefront of her mind. Marie would not win this confrontation. "I expected. Would you like some tea?"

Marie sent a quick glare at Joanna before walking to the foyer. She whisked off her coat and held a hand out for Joanna to take it. "Tea would be fine. Thank you."

So, her mother was going to play the game. Remain composed, act is if this were a social visit. Joanna hung up her mother's coat and moved toward the kitchen. Marie was only a step behind, her voice shrill. "A four year old?"

Joanna sighed. Her shoulders drooped and she quickly resumed a rigid spine. "Yes. Her name's Tracey." Joanna reached for the kettle and tea cups.

"And what has she been doing these four years of her life while no one's wanted her?" Before Joanna could respond, Marie continued. "At least with a newborn it's only what's in the genes, what the mother could have been doing while pregnant, her questionable person, family, etc. But with a four-year-old.

"Look at me." Marie's voice was shrill. Joanna set the

kettle down and turned. "It's ridiculous. She will be damaged, Joanna. *Damaged.*"

"Mother."

"What happened to her parents? Did they die?"

"I don't know. I don't think so."

"You don't know?"

"If they did, that's not why—"

"Then why?"

"Mother." Joanna raised her voice. Marie flinched. "Her mother gave her up, when she was two."

"She wh—"

Joanna raised her hand. "From what I understand she was young, alone. And—" Joanna hesitated. Should she tell her mother more? She'd probably find out eventually. "Tracey was quite sick for a while. It seems the mother was having trouble taking care of her."

"So she gave her away? What kind of person would do that?"

Joanna shrugged, suddenly wanting to defend the woman she'd had the same thoughts about only days before. "A woman who wanted to make sure her child was well taken care of."

Marie shook her head as Joanna passed her a cup of tea. "And the two years in between?"

Joanna motioned for her mother to follow her to the dining room table. A firm chair would do better for this story than one they could sink into. Marie tutted as Joanna related what she knew about Tracey and her past.

When Joanna finished, Marie shook her head once more. "All you've said reinforces how troubled this child must be. Three foster homes didn't want her. Her mother didn't want her. It even seems this group home doesn't want her."

"That's not it at all. It's a policy change."

"Individuals initiate every policy change, my dear."

"By numbers, by practicality—at least in this case."

"Joanna," her mother leaned forward. "Darling, she's a stray. Did you read that story in *The Globe & Mail* last year? About the adopted child who killed her adoptive parents. In their bed while they slept."

"Mother."

"I'm sure they never expected it either. But it happened."

"I'm not worried."

"Well, you should be." Marie sat straight, her rigid spine mirroring Joanna's. "Even if she doesn't kill you in your beds, the sickness, darling. You have no idea what you're getting yourself into."

"Does anybody?" Joanna hesitated. "Did you?"

"What do you mean?"

"You know exactly where I came from. You and Dad can go back generations. And yet you got a daughter with a disease. You got a daughter who married a man you didn't want her to marry. A daughter who is adopting a child against your wishes. No one knows what they'll get. Adopted or no, children are a gamble."

Marie stood. "I suppose you're right." She straightened her skirt. "So, you're determined then?"

Joanna remained seated. But she nodded.

"Don't expect me to call this girl my grandchild."

Joanna's stomach clenched. "Mother."

Marie set her tea cup on the table. "I don't know why you can't just be happy. Some women would consider it a blessing to never have children."

Joanna raised an eyebrow. "Would you?"

Marie reached for her clutch. "I didn't say that." She glanced around the room. "As I said before, you did better with Henry than I thought you would. And he stuck by you, I'll give you that." She returned her gaze to Joanna. "But I couldn't live with myself if I didn't tell you you're making a mistake."

Joanna stood. Her hands shook. "You've told me."

Marie stared at Joanna, then made her way around the table to cup Joanna's chin. A rare, tender motion. "This is for you, darling. I'm only thinking of you."

Joanna stepped back. "No. It's about you, and what you fear people will think. They'll know your daughter isn't perfect." Joanna paused—anger and confusion and hurt racing through her. "Don't worry, I'm sure they already suspect."

"That's what you think?"

"That's what I know." Joanna's heart raced. It'd been thirteen years since she stood up to her mother. Thirteen years. And she was as nervous now as she had been then.

"If you do this, don't ever come to me asking for help. Don't expect me to—"

"I won't." Joanna walked toward the door. "If you don't want to be a part of our lives, you won't have to." They stared at each other. Marie still stood by the table. "You were leaving, weren't you?"

Marie brushed past Joanna. "Yes. I was."

After closing the door behind her mother, Joanna returned to the living room and sank into a chair. Her hands still shook. Absurd, this hold her mother had on her. Absolutely absurd.

She'd been an absent mother, available to clothes shop, to guide Joanna in the niceties of society, but little else. Joanna's Nanny had been the one to fix her lunches, take her to the park, watch her while she was sick. Even to give hugs. But still, Marie was her mother.

Joanna's mind travelled to Tracey. How many hugs had that little girl gotten in the past few years? If things worked out, and they had to, Joanna and Henry would do all they could to make up for it. And not just hugs, but presents, outings, fun. Joanna looked to the clock once more. Still no call. She'd drive herself crazy thinking, wondering. Any number of things could have come up that Nancy would have to devote her attention to. Almost two dozen children, plus a handful of staff, were in her care. Joanna would wait until tomorrow. If she hadn't heard back by then, she'd call.

CHAPTER SIXTEEN

As they were sitting down to breakfast the next morning, the phone rang. Joanna rushed to it. "Good morning. Sampson residence, Joanna speaking."

"Joanna, hi."

Joanna turned to Henry, a smile lighting her face. "Nancy, hello."

Joanna listened eagerly as Nancy apologized for the delay, saying she'd been tied up between this and another case all day yesterday. Dr. Cavell had given Joanna a glowing recommendation. The problem was the court approval. Nancy had called everyone she knew, but they all had caseloads they couldn't push past. The earliest their file would be reviewed was the week after next. Too late for Tracey. And two other children needed placement before then. Nancy was working to find them a foster home, but it wasn't looking hopeful as they were siblings who needed to stay together.

"Which means?"

"It's looking like Tracey will be transferred before this can get pushed through."

Joanna absorbed the words. "Could we foster Tracey until then? Until the adoption becomes official?"

"I would have suggested that," Nancy breathed out the words, "but the qualification process is fairly similar to adoption. The time line would essentially be the same."

Henry stood and approached Joanna, his face coated with concern. He mouthed the words, 'What's she saying?'

Joanna held up a hand as Nancy continued. "Tracey's resilient though. Children generally are. It may help if I told Tracey before she was transferred to the orphanage that a family wanted her, was waiting for her, but as much as I believe this will work out, I can't do that. I've seen too many adoptions fall apart to give her what could be false hope." Nancy took a breath. "Who knows. Maybe she'll really like it there. There's another little girl a few years older than her."

"Most of the children are older?"

"Yes. Most."

"Is there nothing more we can do?"

"Bribe a judge?"

Joanna's stomach clenched. She avoided one on one talks with her father on the best of days, especially if it was to ask a favour. He always had a way of making her feel like a deviant little girl, even when she was doing her best to please him. But this was bigger than that. "I'll figure it out."

"Pardon?"

"Tell me the process, exactly what needs to be done, and we'll make it happen."

Henry raised an eyebrow.

'Dad.' Joanna mouthed.

"I was joking. I don't want you to bribe anyone."

"I know." Joanna smiled into the phone. "I won't need to. Just tell me the process."

Joanna listened carefully to Nancy's instructions. After saying goodbye, she hung up the phone, turned to Henry, and relayed the information to him.

"And you think your dad will make it happen?" Henry rubbed his chin. "He's never been overly fond of us in general." He let out a short laugh. "I stole away his upscale dreams for his baby girl."

Joanna stood straighter. "But I still am his baby girl."

"Do you know what he thinks about the adoption?"

Joanna removed their dishes from the table. "Probably something pretty similar to Mom's opinion."

"He's not that kind of lawyer though."

"He'll know people."

Henry wrapped his arms around Joanna. "He'll be able to do something. This will work. Whether right now or in a few weeks. It's happening."

Joanna bit her lip. She looked up at Henry, her heart pounding. "It's happening."

As soon as Henry left for work, Joanna returned to her bedroom and changed into a more formal outfit. Not business attire, but something she knew her father would approve of. She debated calling his office first. If she didn't, she could wait hours before getting a chance to see him. But if she did, his secretary would likely say he was busy, maybe even suggest she wait until he was home from work—which could be later than Joanna would want and mean Marie would hijack the conversation. So she pulled out of the drive, rehearsing mentally what she'd say. He'd have excuses most likely, reasons he couldn't help. He might be above mentioning the reasons her mother had given, but then he'd have other reasons: he wasn't that type of lawyer, how was he supposed to contact a judge and ask him to put other cases aside to look at hers? Be reasonable, he'd probably say—her father's signature line and one Joanna had heard more times than she could count. She wouldn't accept it today. Sometimes life required that reason be thrown out the window.

After a quick stop at the group home to pick up the documents Nancy said she would need, Joanna made her way to her father's office. Would her racing heart ever settle? She stepped out of the car and to the office's front doors, her heels clicking all the way. The space was clean and modern. It'd been redecorated. Joanna made her way to the front desk, glad the receptionist she'd known since childhood was working today. "Mary Anne, hello!" This would make things easier. The new receptionist her father had hired to ease Mary Anne's transition to retirement was a force to be reckoned with.

"Joanna." Mary Anne's smile was genuine. "Sweetheart, how are you doing? How's your health?"

"I'm doing fine. Just fine. And you, Reggie and the kids? I hope everyone is splendid."

"We're managing, day by day." Mary Anne's smile radiated warmth. "Reggie's so excited to have me coming home soon. It's flattering. Three more months until I fully retire. I'm already down to half hours."

"I know." Joanna rested one hand along the counter. Her foot tapped like a rabbit's. "I'm so happy for you."

"I admit, I'm a little nervous about what I'll do with myself. What the two of us will do with each other. You knew Reggie retired last year?"

"I did." Joanna glanced at the door leading to her father's office.

"And June and Molly are both married now. Molly has a little boy and June, two little girls."

"I got their Christmas cards." Joanna let her smile beam. Was her father just behind that door? "They're beautiful. You must be so proud."

"They're handfuls," Mary Anne laughed—louder than Joanna's mother ever would. She shook her head. "But I love them. Now," she lay her hands on the desk, "what can I do for you today?"

"I need to speak with my father. It's important, so I didn't want to wait until tonight." Joanna leaned forward. "And it's an in person matter. The phone wouldn't do."

Mary Anne's brows furrowed. "Are you all right, darling? I know you've had some health troubles."

"I'm fine." Joanna's heart constricted. What would it have been like to have a woman like Mary Anne for a mother? To receive such a look of concern? To her own mother, Joanna's pains and health complaints over the years had always seemed an inconvenience. "I just really need to speak to my father."

"Good." Mary Anne looked through David's meeting book. "He's fairly booked up today."

"Is he in the office?"

"He is."

"And when's this meeting done?"

"He's prepping for one in fifteen minutes. He told me not to disturb him." Mary Anne tilted her head. "It's pretty important?"

Joanna nodded.

"You go right in. I won't even tell him you're here." She shook her head. "That man. I know he'd make you wait. But it's easier to say sorry than please, isn't it now?"

"Absolutely."

CHAPTER SEVENTEEN

Mary Anne made her way to the locked door separating David's office from the waiting room. After one too many angry clients or "partners" of clients had tried to push through to talk to him, her father decided it was a necessary precaution. Mary Anne squeezed Joanna's shoulder. "It's good to see you, my dear. You should stop in more often."

Joanna smiled back. She knew she wouldn't, and Mary Anne knew it too. Her father's head shot up as Mary Anne opened his office door. "I said ... Oh."

He rested his fists on his desk. "Joanna, hello."

"Hi, Daddy." Joanna didn't like using the term, but knew he preferred it.

"Thank you, Mary Anne." Mary Anne stepped out of the office and closed the door behind her. "Your mother told me your plans."

"That's why I'm here."

He raised an eyebrow. "I'm in acquisitions."

"I'm fully aware. But you know people."

"Maybe one of your brothers—"

"They're hours away, Daddy. It would be different court systems. You know that."

"Paul went to school here. He'd know people."

"You know people." Joanna kept her smile firm. "And you're here."

"I don't see what I can do. I don't see why you're here."

"For one thing, I thought you may want to know more about your soon to be grandchild. First hand, I mean."

"Soon to be? So it's decided."

"It is." Joanna stepped closer. "Well, we've decided. We have all the papers we need, except for a judge's signature. It takes a few weeks ... normally."

"And?"

"And this little girl ... we want the best for her. A few weeks will make it more difficult." Joanna explained the situation they were in.

David came around to the front of his desk and perched on the edge of it. "Policy is in place for a reason. These things take time."

Joanna nodded. "Of course. But favours happen all the time."

"Your mother is strongly against this."

"And you?"

David steepled his fingers. His frown softened. "I want to see you happy. I know you and Henry have struggled." He let his arms fall. "You have a good life, don't you? With Henry. He's kind to you. He provides for you."

"Of course." Joanna stepped forward. "But I want more.

And it's not just that. This child needs us."

Her father sighed, long and heavy. "You think this will make you happy?"

"I do. I think—" Joanna hesitated. "We were meant to find this little girl. Usually I'd say life doesn't work that way That we were *meant to*. But I've never felt something so strongly before. The moment I saw her—"

"Emotions can fool us. Can lead us astray."

"It makes sense on paper too, though. We all know it's not likely I could ever have my own child, even if we kept trying. And trying could be dangerous."

Her father stepped toward her. His hand rested on her arm. Joanna almost flinched, but stopped herself. She couldn't remember the last time her father had initiated touch between them. She couldn't even remember when they'd last been in a room alone. "That last pregnancy ..." His voice shook the tiniest bit. His gaze rested away from her. "I was scared for you."

"So was Henry. So was I. We thought adopting a baby was the answer, but that could be years and years, and here is a little girl who needs us now."

"Your mother." He shook his head.

"Mother said she wouldn't associate with us if we went through with this. Wouldn't call the child granddaughter."

"And yet you're still determined?"

"Entirely."

Her father nodded.

"I could threaten the same." Joanna shrugged. "Say if you don't help I want nothing to do with you, either of you. But I'm hoping you'll help because I'm your daughter. Because this means more to me than you can imagine—making it so this little girl doesn't have to face an additional day of fear and confusion, so she'll know someone wants her."

David drew his hand away. "I see your mother's concerns. This could be difficult."

Joanna's hope sank. "And people will talk."

He nodded. And smiled. "People always talk though, don't they?"

Joanna answered cautiously. "They do."

David's grin expanded. "I don't mind doing something to ire your mother every now and then. She thinks she's more in charge than God. No harm in proving her wrong."

Joanna's mouth dropped.

"What exactly would you need me to do?"

CHAPTER EIGHTEEN

Several days later, Joanna and Henry sat in Nancy's office. Joanna had to remind herself to breathe. Thirteen years. Thirteen years of hope, fear, loss. And now after only three weeks—three weeks in which Joanna's entire world, her entire concept of who she was as a woman, what she wanted, had shifted—she was about to become a mother. Henry's hand found hers. It squeezed. She squeezed back but didn't look over. Her eyes focused on the door, waiting for it to open. Willing it to open.

It had taken work on her father's end, she knew that. He had had to call in several favours. This process, it seemed, was trickier than she'd realized. Her mother threatened to leave him. Joanna had been in the room when she'd spit out the words. An empty threat, of course, and he stood firm.

Joanna could never thank him enough. And her mother, could Joanna forgive her? The distaste she'd held in her eyes, the threat that if Joanna went through with this adoption she might as well consider herself disowned. Why couldn't Marie understand how important this was—more important than what any ladies at the Auxiliary or the Country Club thought.

Joanna tried to pull her mind away from that moment. Her mother was probably being dramatic. A last ploy to save herself from what Marie would consider 'family embarrassment.' If she wasn't being dramatic, though, if she meant those words, then good riddance.

Joanna massaged her hands, her gaze still glued to the door. Her mother didn't matter right now. She may be her mother's daughter in many ways, but not in this one. Henry and she were here, ready. About to become a family.

Today was the day Tracey was scheduled to transfer to the orphanage. Instead, it was the day they would take her home. The door handle turned. Joanna's breath caught. Fear shot through her—could something go wrong? A paper not properly signed. Or worse, would this angel get sick again? Too sick?

But there was no point thinking about that, not now at least. No matter how hard the days ahead may be, Joanna knew this was the best decision they'd ever made.

Nancy's face appeared. Joanna and Henry stood in perfect unity.

"I told her." Nancy's smile sat large. "She's ecstatic. She remembers you."

Joanna finally looked over at Henry. His joy reflecting her own.

"Come on." Nancy motioned through the door. "She's waiting."

They followed Nancy down the hall. Tracey, their daughter, stood in the centre of a small room holding a ratty teddy bear to her chest. Her eyes were wide. Disbelieving. Hopeful. Both Joanna and Henry sank to their knees in front of her.

"Hi," said Henry.

"Hi." Her voice was barely a whisper.

"You remember us?"

The girl nodded.

"And you understand?" Joanna's eyes crinkled. "You're coming home with us. We're a family now."

Tracey nodded, her smile hardly visible. Joanna reached out a hand toward Tracey. The girl's body shifted away. She held the bear tighter.

Joanna bit her lip. Nancy had warned her Tracey had more trouble connecting to women. A greater fear of abandonment perhaps. "Are you scared to leave?"

"Mmhmm."

"You don't have to be afraid," Joanna whispered, keeping her smile large. "Nancy will come visit you a few times. Make sure you're okay." Her eyes misted. "But you're ours now. We're family. And family is forever."

The girl's eyes widened more. She stepped back, distrust seeming to radiate through her.

Joanna wanted to draw Tracey's warm little body against hers, but she held back. If Tracey needed time to adjust, to get comfortable, Joanna would give it. She'd never do anything to scare or hurt or burden this child. Until her dying breath she'd strive to protect her, shelter her from any more pain and hurt than she'd already endured.

Henry leaned forward. "We're your Mommy and Daddy

now. You can call us that if you like, or Henry and Joanna. Your choice."

The girl swallowed. Her tiny throat convulsed. Henry reached out a hand. Tracey didn't take it, but she didn't back away either. "You like ice cream?" The nod was vigorous this time. "And the park?" Her little head continued to bob. "How about we go get ice cream, any flavour you like. Then we'll show you the park by our house, and then, your new room." Impossibly, her eyes widened even more. "With your own bed and toys and name on the door."

This time her smile couldn't be missed. Tracey leapt into Henry's arms. Joanna's eyes watered over. Henry had his girl. She had her daughter. And Tracey had a family.

Nancy stepped toward them. "How about a picture?" She held up a camera. "Your first."

Henry stood with Tracey still in his arms. Joanna stepped beside them, joy pulsing through her. She leaned in close, and smiled.

A NOTE FROM THE AUTHOR

Hello, and thank you for reading *Before I Knew You*.

I hope you enjoyed this quick little story giving a bit of insight into Tracey's (and more specifically, Joanna's) past.

If you did enjoy it, I would be SO pleased if you took a moment to leave your review. Review's are incredibly important to an author's success. You can leave your review at your retailer of choice (such as Amazon, iBooks, or Kobo) or at Goodreads.com.

(Don't know who Tracey is when she's all grown up? Check out the *A New Start* Series. Tracey's story starts in Book 4.)

Thank you!

Charlene Carr

ABOUT THE AUTHOR

Charlene Carr is a lover of words. Pursuing this life-long obsession, she studied literature in university, attaining both a BA and MA in English. Still craving more, she attained a degree in Journalism. After travelling the globe for several years and working as a freelance writer, editor, and facilitator she decided the time had come to focus on her true love - novel writing. She's loving every minute of it ... well, almost every minute. Some days her characters fight to have the story their way. (And they're almost always right!)

Charlene lives in St. John's, Newfoundland and loves exploring the amazing coastline of her harbour town, dancing up a storm, and using her husband as a guinea pig for the healthy, yummy recipes she creates!

Charlene's first series, *A New Start*, is Women's Fiction full of thought, heart, and hopee